CASEY

The OOO Academy

By Amanda B. Reckonwithe

Copyright 2021 Amanda B. Reckonwithe

Smashwords Edition

Smashwords Edition, License Notes

Foreword

What you are about to read is unlike anything you have experienced before, because YOU are willing to keep an open mind! While many books claim to be unique, there is true knowledge for everyone in this tale. Serious readers will be fascinated by the evidence presented while others may enjoy this delightful read as entertaining, comedic musings. As you will see, ultimately in the end, it doesn't matter. So sit back, relax, and crack open an ice cold root beer. Oh, by the way, please don't feed the sharligators!

Howard E. Feltzer-Snach a.k.a. "Bob"

Chapter 1: The End

"All rise!" The courtroom chatter was replaced by the sound of shifting clothes and chairs, and a few soft grunts. I had to elbow my client, Jake Ramos, to get his attention.

"Get up!" I whispered. Jake seemed surprised, but caught on in time to stand before Judge Grossgott breezed into the courtroom from his chamber door.

The bailiff announced, "General District Court of Fulton County is now in session. The Honorable Judge Herman Grossgott presiding."

The judge settled into his high-back leather wrapped chair, looked up briefly with a perfect poker face and commanded, "You may be seated." Everyone sat. It happened like that multiple times during every court session I'd ever attended or participated in. I took comfort in the ritual, the order, even the somber pomp of the judge's flowing, black robe.

The jury had been in deliberations for the better part of three days. It was the fourth morning, just past 10 o'clock, and they were about to deliver their decision. I'd mounted a solid defense and supplied alternative explanations for every piece of circumstantial evidence the prosecution had presented, but I wasn't hopeful. Ramos was guilty. He'd told me he'd done it and was happy he had. I was prepared to assure him that we'd appeal; more a gesture of hope than a bid for justice.

"Ladies and gentlemen of the jury, have you reached a verdict?" asked the judge.

"We have, Your Honor." replied the foreman.

"Pass it to the bailiff, please." The foreman handed a folded piece of paper to the bailiff who delivered it to Grossgott. The judge opened the fold, gazed at it momentarily, blinked once, refolded it, and handed it back to the bailiff who returned it to the foreman. "Mr. Ramos, please stand and face the jury." Jake and I rose and turned obliquely toward the jurists. The judge continued, "Mr. Morgan, please read the verdict."

"On the count of manslaughter in the second degree, we the jury find the defendant, Jacob William Ramos, not guilty." This was not a surprise. The prosecutor had made a strong pitch for first degree aggravated murder. The courtroom waited expectantly. The victim's Mother was glaring at Jake knowing he'd get what he had coming. She snickered softly.

The judge shot her a silencing glance, turned back to the foreman and said, "On the count of aggravated murder in the first degree, what is the jury's verdict?"

The foreman answered immediately, "Not guilty."

"No!!" screamed the Mother. Gasps of disbelief and excited chatter flooded the room. I was astonished, and my face showed it. The judge was hammering his gavel and shouting for silence. The room quieted more slowly than the judge probably preferred.

When it was finally silenced, the judge turned his attention to Jake and said, "A jury of your peers has judged you innocent, Mr. Ramos. You are free to go. This court is adjourned!" He banged the gavel one last time, rose, and quickly exited the bench.

A small smile was on my lips as I turned to Jake and said, "Congratulations! You're a free man!"

Jake seemed a bit stupefied. "What do I do now?" he asked. The Mother was livid, shouting, and sobbing all at once. This trial had been headline news, and the public was firmly on the side of the Mother. Social media had been rife with hatred aimed at my client.

"I suggest we get out of here – quickly!" I grabbed Jake by the arm and pulled him toward a door near the front of the courtroom. Two officers closed rank behind us as angry shouts came from the gallery. I pushed Jake into a narrow, secured hallway that I knew led to an exit at the rear of the courthouse. Two more officers were stationed at the exit. As we approached, Officer Everett said sarcastically, "Way to go Casey. You just put a murderer back on the street!"

"Yeah, yeah, Larry. Just paying the bills." Larry scoffed with a bit of a crooked smile, shook his head, and pushed open the windowless exit door. I saw Jake's head burst into a fine red mist as I felt a gigantic impact on my right shoulder. There were explosions, and the last thing I noticed in that courthouse was Larry going for his gun. That's when everything changed, instantly.

Chapter 2: Bob

My heart was racing, adrenaline coursed through me, yet I was seated comfortably in a deeply cushioned beige chair in a room the size of a generous bedroom. There was no bed though, or windows. There was an ornate, white oval area rug covering a gleaming hardwood floor - cherry, I thought - in the middle of which was a marble coffee table set with cookies, cakes, and beverages. One picture adorned each of three walls, all depicting what I thought were beautiful, yet completely unfamiliar flower arrangements. Strange, but soothing music was playing softly. Double glass doors encased in shiny metal, the kind you might see at a convenience store, were on my right in the middle of the fourth wall, but there was nothing discernable on the other side of them, just the same white light that lit the room comfortably from no apparent source.

I was still in my courthouse clothes, a royal blue Armani suit, cream-colored long-sleeve shirt, and the gold tie I always wore on judgment day. My $800 Gucci's were gleaming like they'd just been polished by Jimmy, my shoeshine guy. But I always skipped him on judgment day, in case I lost. My attire was the only familiarity I could find.

I was beyond perplexed and wondered if I was dreaming, but nothing about the experience seemed contrived. For several minutes, I sat still, waiting for something dreamlike and illogical to happen, but absolutely nothing happened, nothing changed. The music continued to play. My heart gradually stopped racing, and my breathing returned to normal. It occurred to me eventually that I ought to call someone, try to figure out what happened, and where the hell I was. I reached for my cellphone in the left breast pocket of my jacket – but it wasn't there. Now, I'm a creature of habit, and my wife always pokes fun at me about being a little OCD, so I resisted the urge to think I'd somehow put my phone in a pocket where I'd never placed it before. Likewise, I thought it nearly impossible that I would have left it laying somewhere. After a bit of self-argument I gave in and conducted a thorough search of my clothing. The results were even worse. Not only was my phone missing, but so were my keys, my wallet, the ticket from the parking garage, the roll of Lifesavers I always had on me and my beloved Rolex. Damn! I'd been mugged, drugged, and lugged to this weird room!

I'd done some drugs back in college and a fair amount of drinking. I knew what it felt like to be not sober in a number of ways. I knew what it felt like to be detoxing. But my mind was absolutely clear, my movements, so far, unimpaired. I could discern no injuries to myself, felt no pain, had no unreasonable thoughts. I stood and easily navigated around the coffee table to the wall opposite my chair. I didn't stumble. I was not light-headed. I walked to the doors, pushing first one and then the other. They wouldn't budge. Pulling on them didn't work either. Even standing at the doors, nothing was discernible beyond them other than the soft white light. It was as if I and this room were encased in a generous cumulous cloud on a mostly sunny day.

There was little else to do but to return to my chair and continue to consider my circumstances. I was essentially imprisoned. There was no way out of this room; there were no communication devices, and no toilet! What if I have to pee? I didn't, but I was thirsty. There was a large carafe on the coffee table and a single, clear, large, unadorned glass. I picked up the carafe and tried to open the lid to see what was in it. But it wasn't a lid, it was merely the top of the vessel – it didn't open, there was no seam to suggest it could open. I wiggled it a bit. It was obviously full of some sort of liquid. I sniffed the spout but could not identify the smell. "Huh." I muttered. I shrugged and poured a helping of slightly brown carbonated liquid, accompanied by small ice cubes, into the glass. "Maybe this is when I get drugged." I said to the room, and took a sip.

"No man, that's root beer. It's delicious!" I nearly jumped out of my loafers when the man spoke, the glass fell out of my hand and shattered on the coffee table. Root beer splashed onto the rug and all over my Gucci's. He was standing to my right just inside the doors, but I hadn't heard, seen, nor sensed his entering. My wide, startled eyes beheld an average-looking guy I judged to be about an inch shorter than my own 6 feet. He appeared to be in his 30's with medium-length, uncombed, but not wildly unkempt silver hair. He was dressed casually in jeans, sneakers, and a maroon T-shirt. He had a huge smile on his face, and his demeanor put me at ease almost as quickly as his arrival had startled me.

"Who are you?" It was a question, the answer to which seemed immensely important to me.

"I'm God, Casey. But you can call me Bob."

Ten minutes ago, I'd been in a courthouse. Now I was locked in a room with Bob, who claimed he was God. The absurdity of everything was too much. I just had to laugh. Bob looked on with delight as though this was his favorite part. "Yeah, right!" I laughed sarcastically. "And I'm Jesus Christ."

Bob's eyes took on an even brighter twinkle. While still smiling congenially, looking me straight in the eye, he kindly said, "We'll get to that part later."

There was something about this guy and the way he said what he said with such sincerity that stopped my laughter. "Seriously. Who the fuck are you?" I demanded.

"Well, right now, I'm the maid." He glanced playfully toward the coffee table where the glass had shattered. I followed his glance, and was stunned to see that the glass was once again whole and full, the rug showed no signs of root beer, and my shoes were gleaming. Jimmy had never got them to shine like that!

"Holy shit!" I exclaimed. Both my eyes and mouth were wide open as I surveyed the impossible. I looked back at Bob, then back at the table, then back at Bob, momentarily speechless. Bob found my fluster amusing enough to release a hearty laugh.

"Don't worry, Casey. Everything is going to be perfect, but you have to understand some things. First of all…"

I interrupted. "First of all – 'Bob' – you can tell me what the hell is going on!"

Bob was still smiling when he said, "First of all, Casey, you're dead. Think about it."

That was ridiculous. I was obviously not dead. I was having a conversation, and could clearly see most of my body – while not exactly dancing – in obvious animation. Yet, there was certainly cause for pause. The sudden change in venue. Unearthly flowers. My missing belongings. The sudden appearance of Bob. The weird light outside the door. The 'maid service'. But was I dead? I'm having these thoughts. How could I be dead and still believe I was alive? "No, no, no, no, NO!" I persisted. "I admit that something is very different, but I can't be de…" I stopped as the image of Jake's head exploding into mist flashed through my mind. And that huge impact I'd felt. But hell no! I think, therefore I am! I was getting angry! "Bullshit!" I was nearly yelling, "Prove it!"

Bob shrugged, still smiling kindly, and said, "Sure". Bob stepped aside and swept his right hand toward the door. I looked past him. On the other side of the doors was the back of the courthouse. There were at least fifteen police vehicles of various descriptions – all with lights flashing, dozens of officers milling about, and three ambulances with back doors opened. Two paramedics were pushing a gurney out the back door of the courthouse.

A body, completely covered in a sheet, was being wheeled to one of the ambulances. A gust of wind lifted the part of the sheet at the head of the gurney. The head on the gurney was mine, and it wasn't even all there. The right side of my face was completely mangled. Brain matter was well exposed.

I stared in horror as they loaded me into the ambulance and slammed the back doors shut. Officer Everett was sitting on the ledge of a shrubbery encasement, his left arm in a sling. His right leg was being bandaged by one paramedic as another was arriving with a gurney. First aid equipment lay around him, and bandage packages littered the ground. Everett looked distraught and shell-shocked, but was being gently interrogated by a plain clothes detective I'd seen around the courthouse, but whose name I didn't know.

"You're absolutely certain it was three guys, Larry?"

Everett could only nod at first, but eventually said quietly, "I'm certain." The detective nodded, and wrote something on his notepad. Everett became agitated and started talking fast. "I didn't even have time to draw my weapon, Joe! They opened fire the instant we opened the door. It all happened so fast! Joe! I saw Ramos's head disappear!" Tears were streaming down Everett's grief-stricken face. "I felt the rounds hit me in the shoulder and leg, and I went down, too! Then everything got quiet. God! It hurt! It hurts so bad, Joe! I was laying there, Joe, watching my own blood drain from my leg. That's when I noticed that Casey was lying beside me…" Everett trailed off, buried his face in his right hand. His body quaked with silent sobs.

The scene beyond the doors slowly faded until the soft white light once again was all that could be seen. My face was frozen in terror. A soft moan rose from within me. I tore my eyes from the door and looked at Bob who was still smiling kindly, holding my gaze firmly. He placed his right hand gently on my shoulder and nodded as he spoke. "It's true, Casey. Your life on Earth is now complete." I knew it was true. Bob had proved his case. As a litigator myself, I understood that a preponderance of evidence proved any allegation. I had to accept the fact that my body was dead, and that, furthermore, I was currently residing in some sort of afterlife. What's more, Bob clearly had supernatural powers. Could Bob really be God?

With his right hand still on my left shoulder, Bob took my right arm with his left hand, gently guided me back to my chair and sat me down. He took a seat on the coffee table facing me, lifted the glass of root beer, and offered it. "Drink, Casey. You'll feel a lot better."

I blinked several times while looking between Bob and the glass. "Sure, why not?" I muttered and took the glass from Bob's hand. The sweet smell of the liquid was enticing, and I realized I was very thirsty. I tilted the glass to my lips, filled my mouth, and swallowed. An amazing wave of relief washed through me. I quickly chugged the rest of the glass. Refreshment filled my body, and a sense of easy happiness overwhelmed my terror, bewilderment, and grief. That root beer was better than weed! A lot better! The best I'd ever felt was when I kissed Alicia after the minister pronounced us man and wife, but this root beer was even better than that. A smile overtook not just my lips, but my entire face. A sense of joy swelled within me that I was at a loss to explain to myself. I was dead, cut off from the world I'd known. Alicia was no doubt heartbroken, comforting our 8-year-old daughter Brenda. My mother was most certainly devastated. I could feel her pain to the very core of myself, yet the joy remained like fresh sunshine after a violent summer afternoon storm. It was a brand new awareness feeling both sorrow and joy simultaneously. My eyes settled back on Bob's. He seemed utterly giddy, but said nothing as he studied my transformation. All I could say was, "Wow!!" Bob burst into a hearty laugh that infected me instantly, and I joined right in.

When the laughter finally began to wane, I managed to start talking, still laughing between the first several words. "Jeez Bob! I'm so freaking confused! But I've never felt so wonderful! Oh my God! I have a million questions! Are you really God? Why do you call yourself Bob? How can I drink root beer if my body is still on Earth? Why do I even need to drink if I'm dead? Where am I? What is this place? Why am I here? And how the hell did you get in here anyway?"

Bob laughed again and said "Easy, Counselor. Easy! You'll have your chance to 'cross-examine' me." He actually used air quotes, and that cracked me up again! "Everything will become clear in due time. The hard part is all over. When you're ready, we'll begin to unravel all the mysteries of the universe." His eyes were merry, his tone excited.

"I'm ready," I said eagerly. "Let's get started!"

"Slow down, Casey. You're definitely not ready for the secrets of the universe. There are many things that must be explained to you first. Why don't you have something to eat while I take care of some unrelated matters?"

I looked at the cookies piled on a platter next to him and realized I really was hungry! As I reached for them, Bob vanished. I paused my reach for the cookies briefly, touched the table with my left hand where he had sat and said to no one, "Huh. Not even warm." I chuckled and picked up three large cookies. I was kind of excited to see what the sugary confections might do to me considering what the root beer had done. I'd been in the room for what - twenty minutes or so? But the cookies were warm as though just out of the oven. I checked the platter to see if it was a heat plate of some kind, but it felt perfectly normal – room temperature. The cookies smelled wonderful, but the aroma was unfamiliar. My mouth was watering itself in expectation, my stomach gurgled in anticipation. I took a generous bite of one and heretofore unexperienced flavor saturated my taste buds. I rested my head on the back of the chair, closed my eyes as I chewed, and savored the brand new culinary experience. I thought to myself: Man! I must have died and gone to heaven!! When it occurred to me that that was probably exactly what had happened, I laughed and snorted all at once, spewing some of the cookie slurry from my mouth. It landed on my tie, my shirt, my shoes, and the coffee table was once again a mess.

I quickly swallowed what was left of the cookie in my mouth, finished off the other two, poured another glass of root beer, and washed it all down while visually searching the room for a way to clean up the splatter, finding nothing new or useful. An idea crept into my mind that just an hour ago I would have considered pure fantasy. I gave it a shot and said, "Right now, I'm the maid." The mess disappeared instantly. I leaped to my feet, fist in the air, and yelled, "Yes!!" This was very cool! I was stoked! Apparently, the cookies had bestowed at least one supernatural power on me!

I began pacing back and forth excitedly. I wondered what else I might be capable of. What else could I conjure up? The cookies had been immensely satisfying, but I was still hungry. How about a medium rare filet mignon, baked potato with sour cream, and a side of asparagus? I stopped pacing, faced the coffee table, and said confidently, "I'm the chef!!"

Nothing happened. I looked behind me in case the dinner hadn't appeared exactly where I wanted it to. Nope. I was disappointed, but still determined. I stared at the coffee table hard, deepened and strengthened my voice, and commanded, "I am the chef!!"

"It's a miracle!!" exclaimed Bob. I jumped and yelped at the same time. Bob laughed and said, "Congratulations!

You just drove a herd of buffalo into a starving Sioux village in Wyoming in the year 1764." Bob was standing just inside the doors again with the same merriment as before. My surprise turned to confusion.

"What?? What do you mean? Buffalo? Sue? Miracle? What are you talking about?"

"All you newbies manage to perform a few miracles before you're schooled."

I was completely baffled. "Schooled? I've a law degree! What are you talking about?"

Bob grinned playfully and said, "You know, Casey, every lawyer newbie says exactly what you just said."

I sighed helplessly. "Bob, you lost me, man. I…" My voice trailed off as I looked at him pleadingly, shaking my head slowly.

Bob nodded and offered his hand to take. "I was just kidding about the buffalo. C'mon Casey. Let's go for a walk. We can talk." His voice was gentle and those kind, inviting eyes were looking directly into my soul. When I took his hand, a rush of clean love flowed into me. I'd never felt so calm, so safe, so serene. He led me to the doors, and they simply opened as we approached.

We stepped over the threshold into a beautiful, lush landscape. A few steps in, I released Bob's hand, shuffled to a stop, and surveyed the jaw-dropping beauty surrounding me. It was nothing terribly unusual, but somehow different, somehow better, somehow more clean, more natural. It was perfection! We stood on a generous, worn, but not completely bare path that disappeared gently around foliage about 50 yards ahead. A shallow stream ran slowly downhill on my left, the water was crystal clear; I could see the bottom easily and several variety of fish. About a dozen huge oak trees in the immediate vicinity stood like parasols providing shade from the bright, yet soft light. The bluest sky I ever saw peaked between the leaves and gaps between the trees. I could hear birds, and the nibbling and scurrying of squirrels. There was even a moose grazing busily in a small meadow on the other side of the stream. Throughout the scene were single, bunches, and bushes full of incredibly gorgeous flowers as strange as those on the walls of my room. They were somehow all in full bloom, and the combined fragrance was richer than any flower shop I'd ever stepped foot in. It was utterly stunning, it was "Heaven??" I asked Bob.

"Yes," admitted Bob, "but not the one you think it is." Bob walked over to a fallen tree that was large enough to serve as a bench, sat down, and patted the bark next to him inviting me to have a seat. I joined him and noticed for the first time that there was no sign of the room or any building at all. In the direction it should have been was just more of what lay ahead. I was feeling undeniably happy, yet incredibly inquisitive.

"Ok. Ok. I get it." I said. "I'm dead. You're God. This is the afterlife."

"All correct, Casey. Except for the dead part. That's a little tricky as you are obviously not dead, but your body on Earth is definitely lifeless, because your life has been, well, altered a bit." Bob chuckled at his understatement.

"You can say that again! Ok. Well, if you're God, why do you call yourself Bob?"

"Because, Casey, if we all called ourselves God, we'd never know to whom or to which of us we were talking."

I looked at Bob with skepticism and asked "What do you mean – 'we'? You aren't the only God?"

"There is only one God, Casey. We are he, her, it, take your pick." Bob was watching the moose, nodding his head in affirmation of what he'd just said.

That was certainly baffling. "What? Me and you are God?" Even as I made the query I knew it was true. "How can that be?"

"How can it be any other way, Casey? Think about it. God created everything, right?"

"Yeah...."

"In the same way that you and Alicia created Brenda, God created everything. A little itty bitty bit of you, and a little itty bitty bit of Alicia became Brenda. In the same manner, but on a much larger scale, little bits of God became everything. You learned that it was called the Big Bang. That's when it happened. As you know, matter cannot be created or destroyed. All matter is God. We banged ourself and out popped a whole freaking universe with a perfectly balanced book of physical laws that keep it all going, growing, and evolving!"

"There you go with that 'we' stuff again! I don't remember being part of the Big Bang."

"No. Not yet, but you will."

I rolled my eyes, looked to the sky in exasperation, sighing audibly. "This is ridiculous! I am so confused! You're saying that you are God and everything else is, too?"

"Yep. You're God and so am I. Of what else could we have possibly made everything? We were all that existed, but were without form. Everything you see, everything you've ever seen, every person, every creature, every tree, every flower, every planet, star, and galaxy – it's all one thing – God! You, me, Alicia, Brenda, Jake, Larry – all God! That gnarly moose, the cool water in the stream, the majestic trees, the insects, the birds, the fish, the rocks, the dirt, the air you breathe – every bit of every thing – 'alive' (Bob used those silly air quotes again) or inanimate is God."

I laughed at the air quotes, but also with joy. I believed him. I knew what he said was true, but I was far from understanding. My mind was racing with infinite questions, and my facial expression changed so many times as I tried to formulate speech that Bob roared with gay laughter himself. If nothing else, we were completely happy.

Bob stood and started walking casually toward the bend in the path, turned back after a few steps, while still walking, and said, "C'mon! We have things to do, and you have lots of questions to ask! It's time for your cross-examination Counselor!"

How did he know? I'd been planning my assault on the circumstantial evidence I'd witnessed, and I was more than ready for some straight answers. I jumped to my feet and scampered to catch up with him. Once I caught my breath, I started by swearing him in. "Do you solemnly swear to tell the truth, the whole truth, and nothing but the truth, so help you, um… you?" I giggled at the absurdity of what I'd just said, but Bob merely smiled at me and said, "I do."

"Is it true that in the beginning there was nothing?"

"There was no beginning. I have always been and always will be. And so have you been and will be."

I reluctantly nodded in agreement. After all, we were both God. "If I have always been, and always will be, and currently are God, why do I still perceive myself as Casey Dorchester Winsum and have no recollection of any previous existence?"

"Ha!" exclaimed Bob. "I had faith that you would cut right to the chase and indeed you did! Well done, Counselor!" He slapped me on the back in congratulations as we continued to stroll.

The compliment made me feel amazingly good, but I persisted, "That's not an answer, Bob."

He glanced at me with that playful smile and continued saying, "You'll find the transformation goes a lot easier when you let them retain their individuality. When the consciousness you call yourself – Casey – was installed at your conception, your God consciousness was blocked as it is in every mortal. All people are given free will to explore and exist in the physical world until they return to the whole of ourself."

The disagreement of pronouns was driving me crazy, but I pushed on. "Why would you…uh…we do that? If I am God and have always existed, and always will, why would I turn myself into something so much less than that for what – a negligible amount of time in relation to eternity? What's the purpose? What's the meaning of physical existence? To separate the bad from the good?"

"Aha!", said Bob. "Great question – what is the meaning of life! You've heard lots of theories about that, haven't you? You've been taught that evil exists, and that bad people go to hell, and that good and 'saved' (I just couldn't help laughing at his air quotes) people go to heaven, right?"

"Right!" I giggled.

"That's all bullshit, Casey, although very necessary bullshit." I was shocked to hear God curse, but he remained sincere and pleasant. "There is no heaven. There is no hell."

My eyebrows shot up in surprise. "No heaven? Then what is this place?"

"It doesn't have a name," said Bob, "but this is where – or more accurately, when - you discover the things you're discovering. You still have your body and corporeal senses. Your individuality is intact and exists in tandem with your Divine Being."

I wondered what that meant, but continued, "If good and evil don't matter, and there is no heaven or hell, then…the Bible is a lie?"

Bob held his hand in front of him, palm down, fingers splayed, moved it in a see-saw fashion, and said with a doubtful face, "Kind of. Not much of it is true, at least not literally. Same thing goes for the Quran and every other 'religious' document, dogma, and ideal on Earth." Those goofy air quotes again. I reflexively giggled again. Bob was clearly enjoying making me giggle.

"Ok," I said, "so the purpose of life is not to worship you?"

"Why would you worship yourself?" asked Bob. "Remember, you're as much God as I am."

"Good point." I said. "That would be a little narcissistic."

"Mm-hm," Bob agreed. "Vanity. Downright 'sinful'." I saw the air quotes coming, and it just made them funnier, especially with the added sarcasm when he said 'sinful'. We both laughed heartily, and I couldn't help but to admit that I'd never been so happy. My joy was increasing by the minute. I couldn't find a single worry in my mind, but was still incredibly confused. I was God, and I was Casey Winsum. I was dead, and I was not dead. Good and evil don't matter, and good and evil are very necessary. Everything in existence is God, and everything doesn't know it is God. And all religions are bullshit.

"You're blowing my mind, Bob. This stuff just doesn't compute." I was shaking my head with incomprehension.

"Yeah, it's a trip, huh?" Bob was as excited as a kid showing his best friend his new iPhone. "When you understand that you don't understand is one of my favorite parts! You need to ponder on it for a bit. You'll figure it out just like everyone does."

We continued walking while the conversation paused. The trees were well behind us, and we were traversing a large meadow. Two dozen head of cattle grazed to our left, a brontosaurus lumbered in the distance on our right, moving slowly back toward the trees for its dinner. How did I know that? And why is there a dinosaur here? It was a magnificent creature, truly awe inspiring! I wondered what it might be like to be such a majestic specimen of life. Instantly, I knew what it was like, because I had become the brontosaurus!

My gigantic body was the first thing I noticed. The bulk of it moving fluidly below my head was amazing to experience. I felt invincible and unconcerned about what I might trample in pursuing my solitary goal of nourishment. I'm always hungry! My vision was expansive covering nearly 240 degrees. The world presented itself as split, yet overlapping screens through eyes that filtered light quite differently, more brilliantly than ever experienced as Casey Winsum. The delicious oak leaves drew closer quickly as my strides covered more than 30 feet each step. Several birds fluttered about me landing briefly from time to time to pluck insects and small rodents from my hide. I was driven not by logic, but by something more than instinct. It was nearly time to lay eggs, and the need for food was an unavoidable, ancient craving. Good Lord! I was a female!

And then I wasn't. As suddenly as I'd become the brontosaurus, I was once again Casey Winsum, standing next to Bob, my mouth agape, eyes wide in wonderment. "That was incredible!" I whispered.

Bob laughed more often than Santa Claus, and my comment set him off again, which in turn, got me giggling like an eight-month-old baby playing peek-a-boo. Amid guffaws, Bob managed, "I never get tired of watching this happen!"

"Yes!" I exclaimed, still watching the brontosaurus as it arrived at the nearest tree. "I am so hungry! I mean, she is so hungry! No...no...that's not right...she and I are so hungry! Wait..." It dawned on me: "We are hungry, Bob! You, me, the dinosaur, and, and...Holy Shit! The cattle!! I can feel the cattle's hunger, too! Oh my God, Bob! For a second there, I had udders! I know what it is like to be milked!"

Bob was grinning ear to ear and nodding his head excitedly. "Yes, Casey! Yes! You were you, me, the brontosaurus, and the cattle all at once! You're God, and God is everything!"

I was flabbergasted. How was this possible? I mean, like, I got the part about God being everything and me being God, but, "Then why am I not the moose?" I asked Bob.

"Oh, you are Casey. You're the moose, too, and everything else for that matter, but for right now, this small demonstration of omniscience will suffice. You just needed to not just believe, but to know, to be, to experience. It's what God likes to do more than anything else."

I couldn't argue with that. Being all those things at once was immensely satisfying, and I wanted to do it again as much as any addict would their drug of choice. I looked toward the brontosaurus, now munching leaves from near the top of a wide oak tree and willed myself to experience the taste, but nothing happened. I was merely Casey Winsum standing on a path through a meadow with a guy named Bob.

"Damn it!" I exclaimed.

"Not possible." said Bob.

"Huh? What's not possible? God can do anything, can't I?" The reference to myself as God surprised me.

"Of course we can, Casey. But nothing can be damned because Hell doesn't exist. I never created it. It's a myth, contrived by mortal souls to encourage good behavior. Fortunately, the myth also encourages bad behavior."

"Fortunately?" I was dumfounded. "Why would we want to encourage bad behavior?"

"You want people to behave in every way possible. It's how we experience every second of every minute from 7,983,549,116 uniquely comprehended points of view. And that's just the humans on Earth. It's really cool to be both sides of a heated argument and to believe each is totally correct."

"I suppose so!" I said. "Many were the times I wish I knew what was in the prosecutor's mind, or whether or not my own client was telling the truth. But what did you mean by the idea of hell causing bad behavior?"

"Hell idealizes punishment and revenge, a need for which that in my wisdom was installed in humans to facilitate conflict. It is from conflict that we experience the richest and deepest of emotions: hate, jealousy, envy, love, empathy, joy, despair, misery, suffering – stuff like that is incredibly satisfying to experience simultaneously from all parties involved."

That was one doozy of an explanation that instantly made sense to me, because for the first time, I was able to recall the lifeless, matter-less, emotionless being I was before the Big Bang. I remembered the yearning to be with form, with others, with emotion. It had been essential to know what it was like to exist as everything and everyone. I'd wanted to be matter, I'd wanted to matter. All I'd ever known was nothingness, solitude.

But as suddenly as I felt that lonely knowledge, the feeling vanished from me. It was like knowing I'd broken my leg trying to jump Old Man Hennessey's back fence after toilet-papering his house during Halloween when I was 14, but was unable to recall the attendant pain of that break. I remembered my yelps and screaming for help, the ambulance ride, the huge cast with many of my classmates' signatures written upon it, but not the pain itself. I knew it had hurt, but I was unable to re-experience the pain. But just now, I'd gained the knowledge of being a lifeless, formless, insensitive God before it all began. And I knew that even as Casey, I was infinitely more robust a being than my original purposeless state.

Bob had been watching my epiphany. When I finally recovered from the shocking experience and looked at him in disbelief, he placed a hand on my shoulder. With a small and infinitely kind smile on his face, he said "Now you understand why you needed to be you. You understand why there is good and evil, and all the behavior between that abides in mortals. Once you compare life to nothingness, nothing is unbearable. There must always be something, for something is better than nothing. Once we discovered that, then everything became infinitely better than just something. You see, Casey, God didn't create you for your purposes, he created you to be part of his everything. God used you, used and uses everyone and every thing to satisfy the need to physically exist, experience, and effect countless interactions, all of which serve solely to enrich the being you called God and are now realizing you were all along."

I was running out of words to describe my amazement at what I was hearing, knowing, and experiencing. As God, I knew it all to be true, but as Casey Winsum, I was still fighting millennia of human teaching and belief. "But isn't it better to feel love than hate?" I asked.

"Introducing a standard by which to judge emotion was a mortal inclination designed to vilify those who stray from the local prescription for acceptable morality – which is unique in every person. Judgment is strictly a mortal endeavor. God loves all emotions and all actions. Something is immeasurably better than nothing and is the only standard God has. As long as creation exists, God has purpose. God craves existence in any and every way, shape, or form."

My eyebrows shot up with understanding, and I became animated. "So, like…um…Hitler! Right? He was evil! He thought he was some kind of boogeyman and did everything he could to prove it! But that was just you being him so you could feel what it was like to be the most despised human in modern history! And, and all the people he killed, all the people who hated him – they were you experiencing Hitler being a maniac! Right? All the terror! All the grief! All the courage it took to defeat him! And…and…the pride of achieving the atomic bomb! The unspeakable horror of being incinerated by that bomb! The guilt of having dropped it! The relief of having dropped it and stopping the war! The thrill of walking on the moon!

The devastation of 9/11! That was all God experiencing some primo emo!!"

"Yes!", exclaimed Bob. "You got it!! High five!" We both laughed, leaped, and smacked palms!

"Holy shit! I got it! I get it! There IS a meaning to life! Life means I get to experience everything from every individual point of view all at once!" But my elation suddenly crashed yet again, and confusion overwhelmed me. My face screwed up into what felt like a huge question mark. "So…if I'm God and my sole purpose is to experience everything, all at once, well, I'm not doing that. Sure, I got to be a brontosaurus and a cow, and even God myself before it all started - for just an instant – but I haven't been everything all at once. Why can't I?"

"Well," replied Bob, "remember Casey, you were but a single mortal soul – so far as you knew – just an hour or so ago. Giving you access to everything all at once would be, shall we say, overwhelming? No. A better word would be unbearable, at least psychologically. But you're getting there. It won't take much longer – not long relative to eternity."

I looked at Bob askance. "C'mon Bob. Eternity? A million years isn't long compared to eternity! Surely, God can accomplish this…um…conversion?...faster than that!"

"Yes, you can, and you will. However, as Casey Winsum, the newly departed, your spirit must first crawl before it walks and walk before it runs. You had to believe first. You had to know why."

I conceded the point with a thoughtful nod. The oak trees were now out of sight behind us. As we approached the top of a small rise in the wide path we'd been walking, a small complex of buildings came into view about a quarter mile ahead. They were surrounded by a knee-high stone wall of sorts that looked ancient, yet well maintained with groomed vines. It was partially covered with beautiful moss gradient in color from a dark blue to a fluorescent green. Perhaps fifty yards of freshly mowed lawn separated the buildings from the wall. The three buildings were identical one-story structures constructed from the same stones as the wall, but exteriors were clean of vines and moss.

We followed the path that ended at an arch that encased what appeared to be freshly painted wrought-iron doors. "Really?" I asked Bob while pointing at the entrance. "Pearly white gates??"

"A touch of the familiar never hurts!" laughed Bob.

I rolled my eyes, but couldn't stop an escaping chuckle. "So, where's…who?...oh, yeah...St. Peter?"

Bob shrugged and said "Last I heard he was a parakeet in Cancun, but they don't last long, so he could be anything anywhere by now."

His sincerity struck me with hilarity, and I began laughing again which, of course, infected Bob as well. We both collapsed with mirth onto a bench set to the side of the gates. Finally regaining my self-control, I noticed for the first time the lettering above the gates carved into the stone arch.

THE OOO ACADEMY

"Oh?" I asked Bob. He followed my glance.

"Oh! No. It's pronounced ew, like in stew."

"The ew academy? What the fuck?" Confusion reigned the moment once again.

"The OOO academy." confirmed Bob. My eyebrows shot up questioningly, and I shook my head quickly urging more information. Bob laughed again and said, "Some refer to it as The Triple-O Academy. But ew is fewer syllables." Bob sealed his sentence with a wink. I snorted another laugh. Bob feigned a sigh and looked to the sky as if summoning help from above. He looked me in the eye, and with amused patience said, "It's an anagram, Casey!"

I tried to read his mind by staring hard into his eyes, but nothing occurred. I looked up at the lettering again. O.O.O. "The Only Offworld Ophthalmology Academy?" I ventured.

That made Bob roar with laughter. "That's a good one, Casey! But no. It's The Omnipresent, Omniscient, Omnipotent Academy. It's back to school time!"

I looked beyond the gates to the buildings and sure enough, I could make out one of the three words above the door of each of the three buildings. "Oh!" I said with understanding.

"No, it's 'ew'." corrected Bob, using air quotes.

We rose from the bench and walked toward the pearly white gates. As we approached, they swung inward soundlessly. I looked to the left and to the right, but could discern no means of mechanical locomotion. As I stepped through the opening I half expected to hear a glorious chorus singing AAAAHHHHH!, but that didn't happen. Instead, three new paths appeared, one leading to each doorway. Three small signs, shaped like arrows, pointed to each building. The sign on the left read "EVERYWHERE". The one in the middle said "EVERYTHING". The one on the right pointed to "ANYTHING". "That's cute! Which one do I go to first?" I asked while studying the signs and buildings.

Bob didn't respond. When I turned to him, he'd disappeared. I turned in a circle searching for him and calling his name, but he was nowhere. I shrugged and chose "EVERYWHERE". As I walked to the Omnipresent building, I was filled with expectation. Would there be other students? The whole complex looked deserted; not a single soul wandered the grounds. Inside the wall, the grass was mowed like a baseball field, crisscrossing cuts in perfect parallel producing a shimmering green plaid of various shades. The path leading to the door was more narrow than the one we'd travelled to arrive. It was paved with a thin layer of small white, perfectly round pebbles that crunched ever so softly with each step.

Chapter 3: Abby

There were three broad steps leading up to the door of Omnipresent. It was a wooden door that looked like oak to me. I took the steps in stride and reached for the ornate iron handle on the right side of the door. I pulled the door open and just inside stood one of the prettiest little girls I'd ever seen. She looked to be just shy of puberty with wavy, light brown hair that fell short of her shoulders. She wore a light blue dress printed with white and yellow flowers, and little red birds. Pink ankle-length socks and shiny black flats completed her ensemble. Her green eyes sparkled and danced with excitement. Her face was smiling, though her lips were closed. Double dimples made creases that punctuated her mouth like parentheses. She looked familiar, but I didn't recognize her. She waited half a second before she smiled widely, exclaimed, "Daddy!!", leaped into my arms, wrapped her own arms around my neck, her legs around my waist, and hugged me like she'd known and trusted me her whole life.

I couldn't help but return her innocent affection and hugged her as if she were my own child. But Daddy??? Surely this child was confused. Alicia and I had but one child, and unless something horrible had happened in the past few hours, Brenda was still alive and still just 8 years old. This girl was more like 10 or 11. It was a bit of an effort to hold her, but her legs were clamped firmly above my hips which bore half of the load. After several long seconds, she relaxed her hug, lifted her head from my neck where she had snuggled, and studied my face with excitement and joy. "Geezy weezy, Daddy! I thought you'd never get here! It's so good to see you!"

Her exuberance was contagious. I found that I felt an equivalent elation, but was utterly incapable to explain its origin. I didn't know what to say. I was grinning like an idiot; her chaste intimacy was immeasurably pleasing.

There was something about her hair, her eyes, even the shape of her ears seemed familiar. My eyes widened at the possibility: could those actually be my own physical features? With that thought, a wave of joy washed over me that only added to my complete bafflement. "I don't understand!"

The girl threw her head back and laughed gleefully. She drew her face back in close, her smile beaming like a spotlight, wiggled her nose against mine with an Eskimo kiss, and said, "I knew you'd say that!" She kissed my forehead with a loud smack and smiled even more brightly. I didn't get it, but I knew I loved this child. Before I could decide what to say next, she let go and dropped her feet to the floor, took my hand, and said, "C'mon, Daddy, we've got a lot to do!"

She led me through the small vestibule into a classroom. A large blackboard with a chalk tray filled most of the far wall. Naturally, it was low to the floor to accommodate the child's height. Facing the blackboard about 15 feet away was one wooden chair with a padded seat that looked well worn. "Have a seat, Daddy. We can start right away!" She smiled sweetly and turned toward the board. I sat.

OMINIPRESENT she wrote in the upper left hand corner in large letters. Beneath, she wrote: Abby a.k.a. GOD. She underlined Abby twice and turned back to me, dimples still framing her mouth, now closed in that impish smile. She did not speak. I was still at a loss for words, but her eyes – they sparkled and danced without movement. Her gaze pulled at mine and tore my awareness away from the schoolroom. My mind seemed to spin, though her eyes remained crystal clear in my vision. But then, something new was added.

Still glued to Abby's gaze, I saw myself making love to Jenna. We were on the bed in my studio apartment, love songs of the nineties playing softly. It was long after midnight, and we were perfecting our love-making once again, just as we'd been doing for several months by then. I'd worked hard to forget what it felt like to love Jenna; she'd been what I'd considered at the time to be my soul mate. I was absolutely mesmerized as I watched my younger self thrusting into her with carnal pleasure. She gripped my shoulders, her legs wrapped around my thighs, moaning pleasurably with each plunge. I watched as we both climaxed, and just like that, I could also see my sperm rushing into Jenna's egg, my view settling on the one successful little guy. How the hell had that happened? I'd always used protection!

Once the sperm penetrated Jenna's egg, my view zoomed in yet again. I was still seeing Abby's eyes clearly. I was still watching Jenna and I sharing kisses and caresses, but I could also see with impeccable detail the merging of my DNA with Jenna's. That double helix thingy they show you in high school biology? Nope. That would be like trying to describe the inside of the Great Pyramid by describing the outside. I was seeing - along with everything else - electrons merging atoms into new molecules! Millions of merges occurred every second and with each the fabric of life was being woven, a breath of God providing animation to every union. I was transfixed as the DNA zipped up quickly in just seconds. With the process completed, an aura engulfed the egg entirely, then, with a brief flash, was sucked inside the embryo. It was alive! The creation of life was pulsing, stunning, and hypnotizing!

"Daddy?" The voice was as clear as Abby, but I was still entranced with the pulsating embryo.

"Daddy!" She shook my shoulder, and I reluctantly focused on the girl. "Daddy! It's me – Abby!". I focused back and forth from the embryo to Abby, and I finally understood, I knew she was mine. When the knowledge hit, it knocked the wind from me, and the embryo, Jenna, my younger self, the bed, the music - they all vanished. I saw only the schoolroom and mostly Abby standing before me. I looked at her with astonishment, but could only manage a soft sigh of amazement given the little breath I had left.

Abby's face was soft kindness. "Breathe." she coaxed. "Breathe, Daddy." I clenched my eyes closed, sucked in a huge breath, shook my head vigorously, opened my eyes, and exhaled. "Pretty cool, huh?" asked Abby, her eyebrows jumping questioningly.

I let out a horselaugh that made her jump, but also laugh. "Cool?" I said. "Cool??? That was the most amazing experience I've ever had! It was miraculous! Mind-blowing!"

Abby was grinning ear to ear and nodding her head excitedly! "Go on…" she encouraged.

I started talking fast. "How did that happen? How could I be here, and there, and IN there all at once? Why didn't I know about you? Where have you been all this time? How did you do that??"

"It's called Melting." she said. "It's when you suspend the physical laws of time and space. They melt away and allow you to be anywhere, and everywhere, at any and all times."

For a defense attorney, the suspension of laws is somewhat unsettling. I chuckled at my own vanity. Somehow, I knew my former career would be useless here. "Seriously though, Melting? Melting suspends the laws of space and time?"

"That's right, Daddy." said Abby. "God needs neither."

"Right. Ok. Ok. Let's back up a little. How did you do that?"

"I let you piggy-back off of me that time, but you can do it yourself, now. I turned it on for you!" Abby smiled proudly.

"Turned what on?" Is the afterlife nothing but confusion?

"Melting, Daddy! I turned on Melting for you! You can Melt now!" She was nearly dancing with excitement.

I couldn't help but mimic her enthusiasm, but was still perplexed. "That's great, Abby! Thank you! But, um, how do I do it? How do I 'melt' the laws of space and time?"

Abby giggled at my air quotes. "Bob rubs off on everybody!" I looked at my hands still perched in the air, not realizing I'd picked up the silly habit. I rolled my eyes, but she continued, "Just simply want to. 'sall you have to do!"

"Just want to? Just like that, huh? Fine. I want to know why I never knew about you."

This time, the bedroom of Jenna's bungalow on the shore of Old Tampa Bay appeared. It was about three weeks later; the morning of the worst day of my life. I saw myself waking to an empty bed and searching the house for Jenna. I saw me trying to call her several times, then leaving for campus, all the while wondering where she had gone. I had to get back to Florida State for the first day of classes of the second semester, and so did she. I tried calling her dozens of times over the next three days, never getting an answer to my calls or texts. Her friends, Becca and Jennifer, hadn't seen nor heard from her. Her mother hadn't heard from her either and was more frantic than I two days later. We'd called each other several times daily to see if Jenna had contacted either of us.

A week later, Jenna's car was discovered at a motel, along with her purse and empty food containers, but no sign of Jenna. The police mounted a search, but came up empty. I saw myself in a pitiful, drunken stupor a month later, weeping for the woman I'd loved who had disappeared into thin air.

Next, it was five weeks earlier. I saw Jenna, sedated, her legs in stirrups, Abby being sucked out of her, the embryo going dark, lifeless. I watched her awake to the shocking news. I saw Jenna sobbing in that motel room, but I couldn't tell what was going through her mind. I watched in horror as she made her way to the W. Howard Frankland Bridge, walked for nearly two miles with a blank, spacey stare, and climbed over the railing at mid-bay during a ferocious thunderstorm. No one seemed to notice. She stood at the edge for just a moment, then her legs buckled, and she simply fell away. "No!" I screamed in terror. "Stop!"

The Melting stopped on my command. I'd seen it all at once, including the look of sympathy that overtook 11-year-old Abby standing before me. It took a few seconds for it all to sink in. I rose from my chair and walked to one of the windows at the side of the classroom. Outside, the scene was unchanged. I could see the other two school houses, the perfectly mowed lawns, and now there were several Canadian geese pecking about a flower bed at the side of the building next door. A question occurred to me. I turned back to Abby and asked, "So, who named you?"

"I did," she replied. "I am Aborted. Abby for short."

Tears filled my eyes. I went to her, knelt on one knee, and gathered her in my arms. "Oh, Abby, sweetheart. I am so sorry. If I'd known…." I broke down weeping, hugging my child tightly.

Abby returned my embrace lovingly, patting me gently on the back while whispering "Shhh! It's OK, Daddy."

My sobbing subsided slowly as I came to grips with the fresh reminder of the grief I'd known over a decade ago. My mind was doing its best to wrap itself around the most recent events. The shot that took my life wasn't that long ago – perhaps a few hours. I'd died, met God, been God before there was anything, rumbled as a brontosaurus, grazed as a cow, met a daughter I'd never known, knew more about reproduction than any gynecologist on Earth, witnessed her mother's death, and I'd been in multiple places simultaneously. But there was more to the events than words could describe. An underlying joy had grown quickly. The love and laughter was immeasurably delightful. The beauty of this place was beyond description. Most of all, there was the knowledge that I was God, no more and no less than anything else in existence. "I want to learn more!"

"And so you shall!" declared Abby. She walked up to the blackboard, picked up a piece of chalk, and started writing:

MELTING = OMNIPRESENCE
UNIVERSAL
GALACTIC
SOLAR
PLANETARY
INDIVIDUAL
CELLULAR
ATOMIC

My dear Abby turned back toward me and began her lesson. "There are seven levels of omnipresence. Each level may be invoked and stopped at will. When no level is invoked, you will only be Daddy. By the conclusion of this class, you will be able to fluently move into and out of each level, be able to invoke multiple or all levels at the same time, and most importantly, comprehend, appreciate, and incorporate yourself into everything you ever see, hear, taste, touch, or smell." When she said smell, Abby crossed her eyes, sniffed, and wrinkled her nose briefly, but comically enough to make me laugh. She flashed a brief smile, but immediately went all serious again.

"You'll learn how to become an odor, a sound wave, a beam of light, and a flavor. You will know what it is like to be any physical thing, both animate and what you currently would describe as inanimate, though, as you have already had a glimpse of, everything is a frenzy of motion, particularly at the ATOMIC level. On every level, you'll learn to move backwards in time to trace whatever you wish all the way back to the Big Bang. What you will not learn in this lesson is why things are what they are, do what they do, or know what they know. You'll learn that stuff in the next class. Any questions so far?"

"Yeah! Yeah, I have a question. You said before that MELTING suspended the laws of physics and time, yet you're talking about physically becoming stuff and moving through time!" I hunched my shoulders, arms out, open palms up, eyebrows raised. "WTF, my new daughter!?" I suddenly realized I was talking to a child, and my posture immediately turned to chagrin.

Abby let out a burst of merry laughter. "Daddy! You look so silly! Relax. I took this class a long time ago, and I've heard everything. Believe you me – you ought to hear the language that comes out the mouth of a drunken, Icelandic Viking when he accidently knocks over his last cup of mead!"

"Good Lord, Abby! You've heard….well….I guess you have." THAT realization really spooked me for a minute! "Ok, I can get used to that. But, what about the laws?"

"Good grief, Dad. Always about the law!" She rolled her eyes with mock disgust. I chuckled at how mature that sounded, how much like Jenna. She put her hands on her hips and made her voice stern. "You don't call going back in time breaking the laws of physics?? Have you ever even seen a live brontosaurus before? Much less BEEN one?"

"No. Of course not, but when those things happened, the laws of physics remained intact….for everything except ME! Oh! I get it!"

"Bob mentioned you were a little slow." Her impish smile again.

I scoffed, but smiled back at her. My Abby had some sass to her!

"Let's continue." She was all business again. "Think of your awareness as a zoom lens. Finer resolution than an electron microscope can be easily achieved at will. You can even see the space between quarks…"

I interrupted, "Between what?"

"Quarks. They make up electrons, um, sort of like the sections of an orange. They're in protons and neutrons, too. And then, even the quarks have parts that you can see, too, but, honestly Daddy, it's not much fun. I'd rather spend an hour as a boulder than a day looking at quark parts." She waved her hand dismissively with a look of boredom that I found comical. My new kid was quite a character! My gayety was clipped by her next command: "Be an atom in this piece of chalk."

She held it before my eyes, and instantly I could see both the entire piece of chalk and an atom within it. I counted 20 large, neon-blue balls ["Those are protons," said Abby], 20 silver-ish balls ["Those are neutrons."], and itty, bitty red sparkly things whirling about the bigger balls ["Those are electrons."]. It was an amazing sight that I would have assumed to be computer-generated if it weren't for the fact that I was all of them all at once! I could feel the speed as an electron and the pull I had on them as a proton! At the same time, I could see the layers the electrons described in three glorious dimensions, each one independent of the others, but together sketching a perfect sphere. "What am I?"

"An atom of calcium!" Abby was smiling at me with pride, but I was still the atom as well. "Now," she continued, "hold that atom, and zoom out just a smidge." Another sphere came into view. It was smaller with only 6 protons and neutrons. ["That's a carbon atom. Zoom out a liiiittle bit more…"] Another sphere appeared with 8 protons and neutrons at its center ["That's an oxygen atom."] The three spheres were clumped together, touching, and I realized the electrons were actually revolving around all three nuclei. ["That's a molecule of calcium carbonate. Be it!"] And I was! It was literally electrifying. I hummed with energy! This was utterly novel and thrilling!

Abby let me bask in that tiny bit of Godliness for a few more seconds, then said, "Stop now."

Reluctantly, I released the incorporation. For some reason, a news clip popped into my mind – the one where some guy is filming New York City for whatever reason and captured the plane flying into the first twin tower on 9/11. You could hear him yell, off camera, most sincerely, "HOLY SHIT!!!" That was the only way I could describe what had just happened to me, and I said just that.

"Yes!" exclaimed Abby, "Holy shit, indeed. Only God can do THAT!"

After that amazing Melt, things moved much faster as I got the hang of it. Abby guided me through it all, gently encouraging me to zoom out ever more. I became the entire piece of chalk, the blackboard, my chair, and the schoolhouse. I became lumber, glass, shingles, paint, and nails. I saw each thing, from its atomic and molecular structure to its entirety, all at once – simultaneously seeing, becoming, and being everything. By the time we began exploring outside, I was Melting like an expert! I was grass soaking up the sun, digesting carbon dioxide, and excreting oxygen. I melted into every sandy pebble in the path I'd walked, the pearly gates, the stone wall, and the vines and flowers that grew plentifully about. Call me a bee pollinating those flowers. I Melted into what must have been thousands of different insects! As a Canadian goose, I laid an egg and became the egg! It all happened quickly, yet seemed timeless while whenever I was incorporated. I marveled at the complexity, was awed by the molecular architecture, and utterly amazed at the dogged mission of living things to do what they do. I was sap oozing through the trunk of an oak tree, when Abby said, "Stop now. I don't know about you, but I'm hungry!"

I slipped back into Casey Winsum and only Casey Winsum effortlessly, but with an understanding of biology, chemistry, physics, reproduction, geology, and mathematics that a boatload of Harvard PhD's would cower from. I had become things that human beings didn't even know existed and done things that no earthling had ever observed. I had also become seriously famished!

Abby was walking toward the vestibule, expecting me to follow. "I don't get it." I declared.

"Of course we can still eat, Daddy! We're God! God can do anything including get hungry! Now c'mon! Dinner will be on the table by the time we get there."

"Well, then, can't we just be there? Why do we have to walk?"

Abby giggled merrily. "Easy, Zeus! We were human for, well, many reasons, but one of them was to enjoy NOT being all God-y all the freaking time! You can enjoy everything here just as you did on Earth. Whenever it pleases you!"

I was surprised. "God takes a dinner break?" I held one finger up as I considered a question. "Is that when hurricanes, earthquakes, and tornados happen? When God is chowing down?"

"Geezy weezy, Daddy! No! There are like 999 quadrillion of us now, so hundreds of millions are watching everything all the time. It's all under control! Are you hungry or not?"

"Oh, hell yeah!" I broke into a quick walk to catch up with my precocious daughter.

It wasn't a long journey at all, perhaps half a mile. As we crested a small rise, an expansive farmhouse, barn, and fields came into view. I was struck with how perfectly ordinary it all looked. It had to be one of the inspirations that drove Norman Rockwell. Pure Americana, freshly painted white fencing, a weather vane on the barn, sheep in the meadow, and cows in the corn. We walked through a picket gate and up a graveled path to a screen door at the side of the two-story farmhouse. The metal spring squeaked appropriately as Abby pulled it open. "Hey Mom!! Guess who's coming to dinner!"

The woman at the sink wore blue jeans, a red and black checkerboard shirt, and brown cowgirl boots. Her hair was sandy blonde, gathered in a ponytail. She pulled at the apron tie and lifted the neck strap as she turned toward Abby and I. Her countenance was rather sheepish, but she smiled a bit, hung her apron on a wall peg, shrugged a little, and said, "Hi, Casey."

It was Jenna! Shocked doesn't begin to describe how I felt. This was surreal, but made perfect sense. I don't know how I didn't guess it. She was older than I remembered, but just as beautiful, if not more. I'd gone through all five stages of grief when she disappeared, and all over again when I'd Melted and watched her step off the W. Howard Frankland Bridge. Yet, she was here, in the kitchen of this Norman Rockwell farmhouse, walking toward me with her arms open. She drew near and embraced me lightly. I returned the hug, but was hesitant with my affection, still stunned and speechless. My eyes were wide with wonder, my mouth agape. "Group hug!!" declared Abby and joined the family reunion.

"You'd think I'd be used to miracles, by now, but a medium rare filet mignon, baked potato with sour cream, and a side of asparagus was exactly what I've been hankering for ever since I got here." I was talking and chewing at the same time. "Jenna, this steak is perfect! Well, hell, of course it is perfect, right? I mean everything around here is like miraculous! Stuff and people just show up and disappear, the weather is great, I become anything I want, I meet a daughter I never heard of before, and you,

Jenna – never in a million years did I think I'd ever see you again!" I shoveled another large bite of potato into my mouth, took a swig of root beer, and started sawing off another bite of steak. I glanced up at Jenna with a quizzical face, then back at the knife working its way through the meat. "What happened, you know, why did you, um, jump?" I forked the meat into my mouth and chewed while awaiting her reply.

Jenna was clearly uncomfortable. She had said little while serving the food, rarely glancing my way. She got up from the table, took her plate to the sink, and began cleaning it and the pans she had used. She remained silent. "She's a little embarrassed about it, Daddy." Abby explained. "In fact, by tomorrow night, you'll be embarrassed about a lot of things you did, too. Almost everybody regrets some of the things they did on Earth."

I arched an eyebrow as I poked the last piece of asparagus into my mouth. "Well, Abby, that's hardly a surprise. No one's a saint!" Abby giggled. "What's so funny?" I asked.

"We are all God, Daddy! Saints are corporeal and designated by Earthlings before they know the truth! Remember what Bob told you? All that 'religious' stuff is bullshit." Now it was Abby using air quotes, and I couldn't help but chuckle.

"Abby!!", scolded Jenna, without turning away from her work. "You know I don't like that word!"

"Sorry, mom." Abby didn't look sorry at all. I grinned a bit and winked at her in a that's-my-girl kind of way. She blinked twice and flashed that impish smile briefly.

I mopped my mouth with a checkered napkin that matched Jenna's shirt and pushed my chair back from the table a bit. "What an excellent meal!" I declared, determined to lighten the mood. "It was just what the doctor ordered!".

"I'm glad you enjoyed it, Casey." Jenna said softly, but sincerely, with a fleeting smile that quickly fell away. "I promise to make you happy any way I can for the rest of eternity."

That certainly begged more context, but she returned to her chore, her back to us once again. I glanced at Abby with a WTF look. Abby shook her head and simply said, "Tomorrow."

Ok, fine. "So, what's the plan tonight? Do we need to feed the chickens, milk the cows…shear the sheep…or something?" I wanted to be helpful.

Abby laughed at my sincerity. "No, Dad," She raised both her arms, swept them to her left while declaring, "Night school! I rule!!" And, just like that, she and I were back at the classroom.

Chapter 4: Omnipresence

Abby dove right in as though we hadn't just stuffed ourselves at dinner. "Earlier today we Melted into everything within about a 200 yard radius of this room. You learned how to evoke atomic, molecular, and individual Melts of solid, fluidic, aromatic, and acoustic objects. I want you to Melt again into the immediate area. Let me know when you are everywhere. Go!"

I summoned my new-found skill with barely a thought and at once was everything. I was me, my chair, the floor, the walls, the roof, the windows, the grass, the stones, the geese, and even the air I was breathing. I could see the oxygen being transferred to my red blood cells in my lungs. I could feel the color change from blue to red! I was a tiny hair on the root of a blade of grass siphoning water from the soil around me. I was the process turning sunlight into oxygen, not just as the grass, but as every growing form of flora. I was the sound waves emanating from the fluttering wings of humming birds, sparrows, robins, and a dozen other varieties of fowl. I could taste the bugs the geese were eating, and I could experience the horror of being a bug being eaten. I was everything, everywhere, all at once, instantly.

"Got it!! This is really, really cool!!" I exclaimed.

"Well, like the elephant said to the ant that wandered into its trunk, you ain't seen nothing yet! Now it gets interesting! Hold on to your whole Melt you got going. Don't unMelt! You're doing really well, Daddy! The next four levels will come quickly, so hold on to your seat! This will be neat!" Abby was beside herself with animated anticipation. Her twinkling gaze bore into mine. I felt something wash over me, something huge and benevolent. It was more of a sense of expansion than anything else. "You feel that?" asked Abby. Her eyebrows popped twice to accentuate her question.

"Oh, yes!!" I was mesmerized.

Abby broke into a self-righteous smile all proud of herself, and said, "I unlocked the last four levels for you! Ready??"

"I guess I better be! Let 'er rip!" A chuckle began in my throat, but was immediately replaced with a gasp. My view was now of the Earth. A satellite drifted next to me. Instantly, I was that satellite, collecting weather data for the Norwegian Meteorology Institute. At the same instant, I became aware of hundreds of satellites, the International Space Station, and over 78 million chunks of rock orbiting the planet. The globe in my view pulled on me with an irresistible strength. I became the magnetic field surrounding the world and could feel the sun's radiation bouncing off of me. Yet, the attraction pulled me in even more. I became continents, oceans, islands, rivers, and mountains. I was a glacier in Greenland, Thomas Jefferson's nose on Mt. Rushmore, a water fountain on the Great Wall of China. I became every fish, every insect, every bird, every element, every compound, everything. All at once!

Abby had taken my hand, and I could feel her feeling me feeling everything, tasting everything, hearing everything, smelling everything, seeing everything, being everything, everywhere on and around Mother Earth. She let me relish my new awareness for a moment or two. I couldn't begin to understand most of what I was experiencing, and that void annoyed me a bit. I couldn't name most of what I Melted into, indeed, I saw things I'm certain no living human had discovered yet. Still, the certain power I had to become anything and everything was intoxicating! I remembered the Fourth of July fireworks that Alicia, Brenda and I had seen last year in Washington, D.C., which I'd proclaimed as the most amazing thing I'd ever seen. Well, that was no longer true! Did you know that there are dozens of fireworks displays going on at any given moment? Neither did I! They're commonplace! Erupting volcanoes are a lot better. I really liked being magma for some reason. I thoroughly enjoyed its thick, hot and stinking flow, incinerating or melting everything in its path. At the same time, I was entranced by the mating ritual of slugs, the eyesight of an eagle, and found navigating with sonar thrilling and deceptively easy as a bat.

Abby tugged on my hand for me to lean down toward her, and she whispered excitedly, "We are the world!" I glanced at her briefly with a vague nod of my head, my eyes wide, my mind absorbing an infinite number of events with no effort, my self wholly engaged everywhere. "Let's keep going!" said Abby. She squeezed my hand, and instantly my awareness began to expand. The moon came into view and the Earth began to shrink. We zoomed out quickly. The moon became a dim dot. I spotted Venus, then Mars and Mercury. A second later, Jupiter, Saturn, Uranus, and Neptune fell within my purview. There were trillions of asteroids and comets ranging in size from millimeters to hundreds of miles in diameter. Of course, at the center was the sun. I Melted into everything and learned secrets mankind might never discover. I was the solar system! A three-dimensional model of the system you might have seen in a high school science class was no more representative of what I could see and be than a Matchbox Car is representative of a Porsche. I experienced extreme degrees of heat and cold, from absolute zero on frozen comets to millions of degrees at the center of the sun. I discovered that Uranus had a molten core and a water table thousands of miles beneath the surface. Many objects had ice and more than I cared to count had rich microbial populations in their buried depths where the temperature was just right.

An enormous sigh of satisfaction escaped my mouth. Abby was beaming with pride as she watched me experience omnipresence on a solar scale. "Better than sex, isn't it?" she asked.

That question ruined the Melt, and we were once again only in the classroom. I looked at Abby with shock on my face. "How, exactly, would you know that, young lady?"

"Geezy weezy, Daddy, you're still such an Earthling!". She laughed heartily and persisted, "Well, wasn't it??"

I squinted my eyes and looked at her askance, not sure what to say. After all, Abby saw my flashback to her conception, and it made sense that if I could do that, so could she – as me! – hell, as her mother! – Christ on a Frisbee! – as both of us, simultaneously! And, if she could do that with me, she could do it with anyone. I looked away from her and reluctantly muttered, "Yeah. It was better than sex. Way better!"

"I knew you'd like it!" Abby squealed, clapping her hands and dancing a jig. Her exuberance was contagious, and I found myself trying to match her steps and cheering like I'd just won the Super Bowl single-handedly. When our glee subsided, I collapsed onto my chair and said, "Wow! This is amazing! I've already been where no man has gone before!"

Abby had walked over to a table to get a glass of root beer for us each. She came back with them and handed me a frosted mug. "You're not a man anymore, Dad."

I took a long draw from the mug, swiped my lips with my hand, pointed at the blackboard, and said, "There's still two levels remaining: Galactic and Universal. I'm not sure I can Melt that far."

"You can't – yet. Finish your root beer, and then we'll knock out the last part of your omnipresence training." Abby was sipping her root beer and munching on a cucumber. "Drink up, Captain Kirk. Times a-wasting! We don't have all eternity, you know."

"We don't? Why not? Isn't God eternal?"

"Yes, but your training must be completed in three days! I know it's fast, but you're the one that wasted most of the morning in that boring courtroom."

"What?! Like I should've died in the shower this morning?" That was when it occurred to me, "If I'd known that there was an afterlife like this, I might well have offed myself a long time ago and saved myself a lot of grief!"

Abby rolled her eyes. "You would also have missed out on a lot of joy. Grief and joy are primo emo's and the whole reason I created everything! But that's for tomorrow. Let's get this over with." She approached me with both hands held out. "Take my hands, Daddy." Her sweet smile was back.

I took her hands and immediately Melted into the solar system. It happened so fast it took my breath away. There was something new, though. Energy flowed from Abby to me. As large as I seemed to be, I felt myself expanding exponentially. The solar system began shrinking and more stars came into my awareness. "Are you doing this, Abby?"

Abby merely nodded and urged me on with her eyes while still holding my hands firmly, the energy flowing at an ever-increasing volume. I felt the energy become part of me, and my Melt consumed thousands of light years. I was now the entire Milky Way! There were billions of stars, most of which had many more objects orbiting them than our own sun did. I became everything, all at once! The thing that struck me first was the enormous and well-disciplined role of gravity. I could feel how everything had its place, its path, its limit. Everything was ruled by gravity! Secondly, I was hypnotized by the uniqueness of everything in the galaxy. Countless objects from tiny asteroids to gas giants were all different. Nothing was identical in every aspect. Thirdly, I was surprised, and privately thrilled to find millions of planets that supported some measure of flora; some were lushly adorned, others only sparsely. As I Melted into each object with a speed only God could sustain, I found to my astonishment that animal life was present on many, and more than a few supported intelligent life. Sadly, some planets bore the remains of civilizations long extinct. The lives I Melted into were strange, yet familiar. The rules of chemistry, and especially DNA, remained consistent throughout the galaxy. I found a few new elements, but mostly variations of the compounds found on Earth. The people I became were all different, of course, but fairly closely resembled humans. "We ARE all made in God's image!"

Abby merely nodded and urged me on with her eyes while still holding my hands firmly, the energy still flowing at an ever-increasing volume. The Milky Way shrank away. A flood of galaxies entered my realm. Each unique, but all controlled by gravity, chemistry, and the laws of physics. Those things remained constant. I was every star, every planet, every individual, every molecule, every atom of everything in the whole freaking universe!! All at once!!

"Look what you did, Daddy! You made all of that!" She squeezed my hands even more firmly. The universe disappeared. I was surrounded by darkness. I was God before the big bang once again. I was lonely and yearning for substance and meaning. This eternal longing had built up a massive pressure within me. I watched as I exploded into everything I'd just seen, and just like that, the universe once again existed, just as it had a moment ago. I saw creation and billions of years of evolution occur in a blink of an eye, Melting into every morsel of matter and seeing its history since day one. Only God could do that. I did that. I am God!!

Abby released my hands, and the Melt dissolved like vapor from a Juul. She was beaming like a super nova. Pride oozed from her face and posture. My breath finally escaped in a long, contented sigh. "That was…incredible! How is all this possible?" I wondered out loud. Abby was content to revel in her accomplishment and said nothing. "I'd never even tried to imagine such things were possible! So many spectacular places. So many people. So much life. So much death. So much empty space! Why don't Earthlings know about this stuff?"

Abby finally spoke. "It would ruin everything if people knew that other people existed on other worlds. Check it out, Dad, now that you've been everywhere – did you see anything that resembled an interstellar space craft? Did you see any references in libraries, monuments or broadcasts to life existing beyond any planet you saw?"

Amazingly, I was able to retrieve everything I'd seen and become instantly, even without Melting. Nowhere in that data was any hint that anyone on any world was aware of life on any other planet. I'd seen some local space traffic around planets with more intelligent life, but there had been no vehicles traveling between stars. "No. Nothing at all! WTF, Abby! No one has figured out how to travel faster than light? Why not?" I was genuinely disappointed.

"Tomorrow.", said Abby. "Day two is a doozy! But Daddy – Congratulations! You have successfully completed the Omnipresent module of your training! And you did SO good! I'm really proud of you!" She leapt into my arms and hugged me tight, her head nestled between my neck and shoulder, once again simply my child. We held the embrace for several moments, neither of us wishing to part. I'd never felt love like this, so pure, so innocent, so safe and sincere. Reflecting on this day, I couldn't help but to consider that dying wasn't nearly the horror I'd always imagined. While eating my Grand Slam Breakfast this morning, little did I know that before sunset I'd have seen and been the entire universe. Nor could I have imagined falling in love with a child more deeply, more profoundly than I had with Abby. She and I had shared an experience that no father and daughter on Earth could ever come close to. I wondered if I would be able to do for Brenda what Abby had done for me when her time came. As much as my love for Abby shone brightly, it saddened me profoundly that I might not see Brenda again for quite some time.

The light outside the classroom had taken on a hint of duskiness. The sound of crickets, frogs, and other nightlife was beginning its nightly crescendo. I realized I was rather worn out. After all, I'd been to the edge of the universe and back. Though it hadn't taken even an hour, that's a lot of traveling for one day! "So," I said, "where do the newly departed bunk around here?"

"Departed?? You're silly, Daddy! You are one of the newly arrived! And newbies sleep on campus the first two nights. After that you can….well, you'll see!" She flashed that impish grin again and walked over to a door at the side of the classroom. "You'll find everything you need right in here." She opened the door to reveal a spacious, yet cozily decorated bedroom. It held a generous bed with a fluffy comforter and two pillows, a nightstand on which there was a pitcher of root beer, two glasses, and a bucket of little ice cubes. There was also a plate with four Pop Tarts on it. "They're you're favorite Dad – blueberry!"

I had to laugh at her childish enthusiasm. "Awww, you're so sweet, Abby! How'd you know?"

"I'm God. I know everything." She smiled sweetly, then vanished.

Chapter 5: Omnicience

The crowing of a rooster woke me the next morning. I lay there regaining my wits after a dreamless sleep. It took me a moment to realize where I was – and why! I wouldn't be kissing Alicia good morning, dropping Brenda off at school or having breakfast at Denny's today. I wouldn't be going to court today. I wouldn't be bringing a coffee to Jerry, the parking garage attendant. I wouldn't be worried about my diabetes today. I wouldn't be getting angry about the snail's pace at which the legal system moved. Today, I was going to make like Rodney Dangerfield and go back to school! Recalling yesterday's lessons, I was more than eager to discover what today would hold.

Two and a half Pop Tarts remained on the plate, and I'd only drank about half a glass of root beer before stripping out of my lawyer duds (leaving them on the floor – a habit that thoroughly annoyed Alicia) and crawling into bed last night wearing nothing but my boxers. Sitting on the edge of the bed, I finished off the pastries and guzzled two glasses of root beer. I hoped I'd see Abby again today. I missed her terribly already. Standing up, I searched the room for my clothes, but they were nowhere to be found. I did find a closet with a variety of casual wear in my size, and the dresser at the side of the room was filled with underwear. Yesterday, this alone would have stunned me, but today, it only drew a "Huh!" from me. I selected a green polo, white slacks, a pair of tube socks, a pair of brown loafers from the closet, and dressed myself quickly. I was eager to get on with my training!

With a final inspection in the mirror attached to the dresser, I smiled and winked at myself. I opened the bedroom door and walked back into the classroom. But this classroom was quite different. Looking out the windows I could see buildings on either side. The one on the left was the OMNIPRESENT building, the one on the right, the OMNIPOTENT school. I deduced that this must be the OMNICIENT schoolhouse. There was whiteboard this time, but it was higher on the wall, placed for an adult. The room looked more like a hotel lobby, only much smaller. Comfortable chairs and sofas were placed around. A buffet was on one wall, with steaming trays of breakfast food. A large coffee urn attracted me immediately, and I walked over to make myself a cup. As I was stirring in the cream and sugar, I heard someone enter from the front of the room. "Abby? Is that you?" I called. No reply, but the footsteps continued toward the whiteboard. By the time I turned around, the woman's back was toward me, and she was writing on the whiteboard.

OMINISCENT she wrote in the upper left hand corner in large letters. Beneath, she wrote: Jenna Henson a.k.a. GOD. She underlined her name twice. "Have some breakfast, Casey. I'll be ready when you are." she said without turning her face to me. She continued writing.

Jenna! Holy instructors, Batman! Of all the people in heaven(?), Jenna was to be my omniscience trainer? This could be awkward! But I went with it. I took a plate and began filling it with pancakes, sausages, bacon, and grits, all the while glancing back at Jenna as she continued to write. I sat in one of the plush chairs that wasn't far from the whiteboard, set my plate on a square table that sat in front of it and began eating as I watched her fill the board.

CERNING = OMNICIENCE
TO BE IS TO KNOW
TO KNOW IS TO FEEL
THOUGHT BEGETS EMOTION
EMOTION IS LIFE
LIFE IS GOD, GOD IS LIFE
I AM GOD AND SO ARE YOU

INANIMATE   ANIMATE   CONSCIOUS
CONSCIENCE

IT DON'T MATTER

The Pop Tarts had only served to whet my appetite,
and I'd woofed my breakfast down quickly. Jenna finished
writing just as I was popping the last bite of sausage into
my mouth. She was dressed in colorful business attire,
yellow blouse, blue pencil skirt, and a red blazer. Her hair
was gathered behind her head in a bun held by a modest
metal pin. She finally turned toward me, smiled ever so
slightly, and asked, "Shall we begin?"

I pushed the table back a bit and settled into the
comfortable chair. I shrugged and said, "Sure. Lay it on
me, Babe!" My ploy at familiarity was ignored, and I
found it a little annoying. Instead, she assumed a tone that
immediately reminded me of Professor Gingrich in
Constitutional Law as she began her lecture.

"Thousands of religious authors have professed to
write down words somehow delivered to them from, or
inspired by a Supreme Being. Billions devoutly believe
those words. The veracity of all those words was
determined by thousands of mortal men throughout history;
still edited and tweaked today for consumption by under-
informed humans.

"At the heart of every religion is the struggle between
good and evil. Good is generally defined as those
characteristics of thought and behavior which serve to
prolong, enhance, and improve the enjoyment of life.
Conversely, evil seeks to shorten life, make it miserable or
end it altogether.

"Naturally, religions promote the good stuff with their
Supreme Being of choice as the final judge of individual
success. People live their whole lives trying to be good and

asking forgiveness for when they are bad. People are taught to pray to their Supreme Being, as though such solicitation could change the behavior of other people, animals, inanimate objects, Mother Nature, and the Universe, to name a few.

"We are taught that our Creator is omnipotent, omniscient, and omnipresent. We learn that the Creator is NOT us, but something separate and immeasurably more powerful than any single human being. There is a kernel of truth to every story. Let's see how it all began....

"There is ONLY God. God was, is, and always will be. Because God was lonely and bored, God decided to create everything. Naturally, Creation was made from the substance of God. After all, nothing else existed yet. Just as human biological matter is required to make humans, God matter is required to make Universes. Everything you see, feel, touch, smell, and taste was made wholly from the matter of God. In our Universe, matter cannot be created or destroyed, just like God.

"God created our physical laws to provide for a self-sustaining, infinite evolution of God's matter. Dust to dust and all that. From the smallest quark to the most gigantic stars – and everything in between (including nothing)- it all consists exclusively of God matter.

"As do I. As do you. As does everyone and everything there is. Within everything, each tiny bit of God matter contains every bit of what God is. However, each bit of matter only manifests that portion of God which events and environment bring to pass by virtue of a symphony of evolutionary paths, unique to every bit having forbearance.

"This evolution of matter occurs at every level, from invisible micro-particles to compounds, to biological systems, immune systems, ecosystems, solar systems, galaxies, and universes. They all start as God, evolve as God, and return to God only to be utilized to create more stuff. After all, that's what a Creator does: manufactures stuff that didn't exist before.

"In a physical sense, it is easy to allow that I and You, and everything else IS God. There was nothing else, but God, from which to create everything.

"God, therefore, created Man; the result of billions of years of evolutionary complexity, originally made inevitable by the Creator's infinite Wisdom at the time of the "Big Bang".

"How Mankind got here and that we ARE God is fundamentally obvious, given our current knowledge of the physics of our universe. God created evolutionary systems, powered by DNA, RNA, and chromosomes, that ultimately resulted in our current evolutionary situation – that of being the most self-aware, intelligent living thing on Earth.

"This happenstance was not accidental, but rather inevitable. God is not only every physical thing, but every physical thing is comprised also of God's character as well. God's character is infinitely robust. It spans the entire gamut from evil to good. God created everything, including intentions and the lack thereof. A rock has no intention, but may manifest its evil by crushing your skull should you contact it at a high enough rate of speed.

"God's Creation necessarily evolved to endow Mankind with a brain capable of complexly analyzing God's Creation and to ask all the questions thereof. It is that consciousness that is a character version of GOD. Some of us are very evil, and some of us are very good. Everyone is capable of both, but evolution and environmental factors created by God cause each of us to manifest a fairly narrow character comprised of both good and evil.

"Evil is a term wrought with mental pictures of demons, death, fire, hell, damnation, etc., but there is no evidence in Creation that demons, the devil or damnation exist. Hell is a concept designed to control the evil part of

God that dwells within each of us. Likewise, Heaven is the concept reserved as a reward for good behavior. What a helpful thing to believe! But those places do not exist, and they do not need to exist.

"God's goal in creating Mankind was not to run some kind of moral experiment. Mankind has behaved immorally since we've been able to track our history. It seems rather psychopathic to create so many people, only to send the vast majority of them to Hell. Would you send Abby or Brenda to Hell? Your children are just as much you and I and God as they are everything in Creation, The concept of Heaven seems equally pointless, if not eventually boring and worthy of suicide.

"So, why ARE we here? Before Creation, God was sensory deprived. We are God experiencing Creation. God wanted to see, hear, smell, touch, and taste everything and everybody created. God set everything in motion, with built-in obstacles, perils, and rewards. As each individual, God responds to Creation uniquely; sometimes helping, sometimes hindering. The bad things that happen allow God to experience grief, sorrow, hatred, tears, depression, and sadness. The good things that happen allow God to feel happiness, joy, elation, and love. God experiences BOTH sides of every conflict, every celebration, every defeat, every victory. God is us, and we are all about senses.

"All this talk about good and evil is irrelevant. When our body dies, our soul/mind/consciousness returns to God, and our self-awareness quickly transforms into the all-awareness of God being everyone still 'alive' as well as those who have "died". God's all-awareness requires the self-awareness of each of us, necessarily pruning our awareness to only our physical senses and a vaguely nagging thought that we cannot imagine our own beginning and find an ending completely irrational. THAT thought is the TRUTH.

"We have no beginning or end because we are God. Ergo, behavior while "alive" is inconsequential to the 'afterlife'.

"God set each of us with a mind. A mindset. Each designed to produce all manner of experiences with other intelligent beings. As each of us performs according to our unique mindset, God experiences Creation as each of the people with whom interaction occurs. The point is not WHAT we do, but that we simply DO what we do. Being alive allows God to experience Creation, not just from within you, but also from the viewpoint of everyone with whom you interact.

"Because mindsets run the gamut of evil to good, neither side will ever prevail indefinitely. The line dividing good from evil cuts through every mortal's heart. History is replete with examples. This balance ensures indefinite preservation of the experience of both good and evil, and everything in between. That is our goal, God's goal – experiencing life and all the emotions it delivers."

Jenna stopped talking and simply looked at me as if I had something to say. I wanted to say a lot, but was struggling to pick one thing. At last I simply dove in. "But that didn't happen yesterday when I was Melting. I became everything, including a shitload of aliens, but I didn't feel any emotions from them. I couldn't discern their motivations."

"That's what you will learn how to do today with my help. You will learn how to discern. It's called Cerning." She pointed to the word on the board. "When you Cern, you instantly tune in to the entire current mindset, physiology, and psychological history of an intelligent being, or, if Cerning an inanimate object, you tune in to its evolutionary history and environmental impact. Cerning is much like Melting in that you can adjust your focus to a single object or person, or include whatever or whoever you want up to and including the entire universe. Simultaneously, of course."

"Of course." I confirmed, trying to imagine not just being but knowing a bunch of people in a way they would find invasive.

"Don't worry, Casey, mortals cannot detect your Cerning any more than they can detect your Melting. Neither will change or affect them in any way."

"That's a relief." I said. "But, I'm not so sure I want in the heads of some people!"

"Oh, you'll want to, alright! In fact, it's utterly addicting. It is our purpose. To know all, to feel all. It's why I created everything. As God, it is our oxygen. There is no point to existing if there is nothing to observe. Anything is better than nothing."

"Yeah! That's what Bob sled, I mean said!" trying to lighten the mood.

Jenna ignored my malapropism and continued on professorially. "You will begin your training today by Cerning an inanimate object, anything that is not alive, cannot move, doesn't reproduce, and has no brain whatsoever. Let's start with that chair you're sitting on."

"Sounds like as good a thing as any for my first Cern. So, how do I Cern?"

"Cern that chair!" commanded Jenna.

Instantly, I Melted into the chair, as I might have done yesterday. I could see every atom, molecule, compound, and bits of debris. I immediately understood every detail of its construction, just like yesterday. But something new was happening! I saw trees being cut into boards, hide being stripped from animals, and stuffing being spun in a factory. I watched the chair being built, bagged, shipped, and delivered to this very room. Then, incredibly, I could feel my weight on it. I sensed its resolute determination to remain whole and sturdy. It was proud to be strong and comfortable, content to be what it was – a restful servant to bipeds.

"Stop!" commanded Jenna.

"Whoa, buddy! That was fantastic! How did I do that??"

"I facilitated the merging of your Godness with its. The energy that oscillates in its atoms is the same energy that is God. I removed your mortal block momentarily to allow your energy to merge with that of the chair. As we continue, you'll become more efficient, and by this afternoon be capable of invoking a Cern whenever you wish. Now, Cern that coffee urn!"

I looked toward the urn, and the instant my eyes landed on it, I saw magma spurting from a volcano and flowing down its slope. I saw it cool over millions of years and be covered by more and more layers of magma, sediment, and soil. I watched as the ore was mined and purified into sheets of aluminum. Huge machines shaped, cut, and welded the sheets into the body of the urn. Workers assembled it, boxed it, and placed it on a pallet with others. It was shipped, delivered, and plugged in. Electricity flowed into its electronic components. The urn was impervious to the acidic nature of its content, and I sensed the same pride of singular purpose and service I'd experienced with the chair.

"Stop!" commanded Jenna.

I was beginning to get really excited about Cerning! To know what it is to be a coffee urn was completely satisfying. "Why'd you pull me out?" I complained.

Jenna flashed a smile for the first time, but it faded quickly. "We're just sampling right now. Trust me, there will be plenty of Cerning for you to enjoy soon enough." She walked over to the buffet, picked up a vase of flowers, and brought it to the table in front of me. "Cern this daisy!" she commanded, pointing at one of the blooms.

I was a seed bursting from absorbing moisture. I had an irresistible urge to grow! I put out roots to suck up water and nutrients from the soil, and built new molecules at an astonishing rate. I burst through the soil into sunlight, and my strength improved by ten-fold. I soaked in sunlight and manufactured chlorophyll. Still growing and developing new cells, I found myself developing buds and knew that beauty was just hours away! Then, at last, my bloom opened, and I proudly displayed my attractiveness for all to partake. Bees were my friends. Then, someone cut me! Oh! The pain!! My lifeline to the soil was severed! I will wilt and die! But not yet, I've been placed in water with many other plants and flowers, more beautiful than ever. I bring pleasure to all who see me.

"Stop!" commanded Jenna.

"Wow! That was different! It was like I was actually the flower itself!"

"Yes," confirmed Jenna, "That's the difference between ANIMATE and INANIMATE." She pointed at each word on the whiteboard as she spoke them. Animate objects contain God energy just as inanimate objects do, but, by virtue of that daisy containing God's will to live as well, we are able to personify the Cern."

"If I hadn't just experienced it, I would have said it was unbelievable! This is absolutely remarkable! I love this animate Cerning! Can we do more?" To my astonishment, I found myself yearning for more Cerning! I was jonesing like a smoker who ran out of cigarettes four hours ago.

Jenna's countenance was more satisfied now, but her manner remained professional. "Certainly, and necessarily. Next, we'll do CONSIOUS." She pointed at that word on the board. "Conscious animates are living things with brains – everything from insects, to birds, to reptiles, to fish and every animal that is not intelligent, like cows, moose dogs, cats, mice, etc.."

"Oh! I remember this part! When I was with Bob, I got milked!"

Jenna furrowed her brow for a moment and looked away. Then her face cleared, and she said "Yes. Well, that was just a snapshot. This time I want you to Cern the cow."

"What cow?" I asked, looking around the room quickly. I wouldn't have been surprised to find one standing behind me, but the room had no cows.

Jenna rolled her eyes and let out an exasperated sigh. "Newbies!" she muttered under her breath. To me she said, "Honestly, Casey, did you not pay attention yesterday? Cast a Melt, and find a cow! Jeezy weezy!"

Well, that explained Abby's vernacular. "Oh. Yeah. Sorry, Jenna. Let me see here…OK! Got one now – ohmagod! I'm in!" In no more time than it takes a motor to complete a single revolution at 5000 RPMs, I was an inseminated embryo, grew into a calf, was born and spent hundreds of days munching grass in a meadow. My name was Buttercup. Every evening, I'd make a slow, lumbering stroll to the barn, sleep standing up, and every morning I got milked. I really enjoyed the tugging on my teats and the ultimate relief it provided. I was content to be what I was and took pleasure in the routine and product I supplied. At the moment, a bull was sniffing around me, and I felt a little skittish while being attracted to it at the same time.

"Stop! Stop!" Jenna was a bit unsettled. I even chuckled at the horror on her face. She took a moment to gather herself and said "You would pick a cow in heat! Just like a man!"

Where did this resentment come from? I felt a strong urge to Cern into Jenna right then and there, but I couldn't quite evoke it myself. I wanted to know why she was so angry. God knows everything. I am God. I want to know!! Dammit. "Well, excuse me! I didn't know until I was in there!"

Jenna shot me a withering glance, but her face softened quickly enough. "Never mind. It's all good." She went over to the buffet and fixed herself a cup of coffee. "You want one?" she asked.

"Sure. Three creams, one sugar."

"I remember." she said quietly. She brought the cups over and handed me mine. She sat down in the chair next to mine and sipped at her coffee without speaking. She seemed to be ignoring me. I took advantage of the pause in training to exercise my new skills. To my surprise, I found that I could Melt and Cern into everything in the room, except for Jenna. While it was still novel and captivating, Cerning into inanimate objects produced surprisingly similar results. Everything started out as a natural resource which was harvested, manipulated, manufactured or processed, and delivered. Inanimates were always content to be what they were. I finished exploring every lifeless thing in the room in a minute or so. Jenna was still sipping and staring out a window, her gaze a thousand light years away. I continued to survey the room. I Melted and Cerned into other plants and flowers in the vase. The remaining breakfast food on the buffet was a little interesting. I could have done without seeing how many different DNA's were in a sausage link, and it was fascinating to see how wheat was processed into flour. I was even able to track the history of wheat and learned over fifty distinctively different ways to mill it. I'd learned more about manufacturing and processing in the last thirty minutes with Jenna than I'd learned in an entire lifetime on Earth.

Jenna remained quiet and pensive, apparently lost in thought. I mentally shrugged and continued my exercises. I jumped into an ant, a spider, and a whole lot of other bugs who didn't even know what they were themselves, but I marveled at their efficiency of movement and engineering skills. I stayed in the spider several seconds – a long time for a Cern – hypnotized by my skill and artistry as I spun a web. There were no blueprints or instructions to work from, I simply did it as easily and mindlessly as one ties a shoe. It was a bit disturbing to understand the craving I had for a nice, fresh, juicy fly! Every insect had but three imperatives: find food, reproduce, seek shelter from prey. Yet, each bug had a secondary mission that serviced the environment. I'd always thought that roaches were dirty, nasty looking things, but they were accomplished sanitation engineers. If there was so much as a whiff of food in a dark place, they cleaned it up in practically no time. They'd been doing just that since before there were dinosaurs. I understood that if one is willing to eat anything, one could also survive nearly anything.

All animates into whom I Cerned held one priority above their imperatives: to stay alive. And yet, there was a sense of mortality in all I surveyed. Every living thing knew it would die, no matter what. That knowledge motivated them to be what they were as long as they could, because they also had a sense of purpose and an obligation to not waste their brief livelihood.

Having studied everything in the room, I decided to cast my Melt beyond the room to the campus grounds and immediate vicinity. I was exhilarated to find that I could Cern beyond the classroom! I learned what it was to be thousands of different plants, hundreds of various bugs, over thirty different birds, five species of fish, two kinds of frogs, and that moose I saw while walking with Bob. I surveyed everything in a matter of moments and learned a thousand times more stuff than I had in three years of law school. Moreover, I gained the knowledge of being each and every thing. Amazingly, as I learned, I found that my attention was never exclusive, and every fact made known to me stayed within immediate recall. I could be transfixed by the eyesight I had as an eagle while enjoying the satisfaction of laying eggs as a chicken. My appetite for knowledge was becoming a beast of its own. I couldn't seem to Melt and Cern fast enough! I cast my Melt another thousand yards out from the campus.

"Ok! That's enough of that for now." Jenna had come back to life and was walking to the whiteboard. My Melt vanished before I could try to Cern anything.

"Ah, c'mon, man! I just found a tortoise! I want to know what it is like to be a tortoise!" I complained.

Without turning toward me, Jenna waved a dismissive hand and said, "It's not all that different from a frog. You'll have plenty of time to expand your knowledge of animates after graduation. Today, we must continue your lessons." She'd reached the whiteboard by then, picked up a marker, and underlined CONSCIENCE. When she turned back to face me, she was clearly nervous. "This next level of Cerning is what drives everything. When you've completed this exercise," a slight cringe over took her face, "you will understand why God created the universe." Her face settled a bit, and she continued, "Conscience, for our purposes, means intelligence, self-awareness, and variable intention. On Earth, only humans have conscience. Humanoids on other planets do as well. Conscience is supplied by God, from God, and therefore, is God. Every sentient being is a tiny, unique, highly abridged, but complex fragment of God. Conscience is responsible for every thought, every intention, and, therefore, every emotion, good, bad, or indifferent. When you Cern into a conscience being, you literally become that being. You think as they do, act as they do, and feel as they do. It's not vicarious. It's…" She paused, searching for a word, "miraculous, and utterly addicting."

"You're talking about becoming other people?" I asked.

"Yes, anyone, anywhere, at any or all times of their physical life." she answered.

"You mean, like, I could Cern into, say Ronald Reagan?"

"Yes, I have, and you will, too. In fact, once practiced, you'll be able to Cern into the physical life of every sentient being that has ever existed, anywhere, simultaneously, if you wish, or just one or a few at a time. You'll spend a large part of eternity doing just that. It's what God craves. It's what God needs. It's why everything exists."

"Imagine that!" I exclaimed, "I can be anyone? Everyone? All at once??"

"Yes, but not so fast. Becoming another is quite shocking and mind-blowing. We'll start with just one person." Her voice trailed off on the last two words. She quickly clenched her lips in a grimace and squeezed her eyes shut for a moment. After a few seconds the malaise cleared, and she looked at me with an expression I'd never seen before – on anyone. It was subtle, very subtle, but it was fear, just below her tranquil surface.

Was I reading her correctly? Maybe she just had gas or something. Every minute I'd spent with her the past two days, she had been very different from the Jenna I'd fallen in love with so many years ago. She seemed cool, detached, and off-putting. Her dispassionate delivery of her lesson today was entirely incongruent with the Jenna I'd known. My concern softened my voice, "Ok, Jenna. That's fine. We'll start with just one person. But there's no one else here. Should I Melt and find someone?"

"No, Casey. There is someone here." Her eyebrows rose urging me to solve the simple riddle, and her fear broke the surface.

I didn't get it. "Who!?" I quickly swiveled my head in all directions to see if Hitler or Attila The Hun had popped in. Whoever it was, Jenna seemed terrified.

With false bravado, Jenna walked to within a foot of me looking me straight in the eye. She was trembling now.

She took my hands into hers, her face begging for mercy, and stuttered, "M-me."

Chapter 6: Jenna

The difference between Cerning into an object or animal without conscience and one with conscience could not be more profound. With everything else, there is no memory, and there is no expectation of the future, at least not beyond a few minutes in some of the mammals. While I could see and feel the history of non-conscience bearing objects, there was no sense that that history had any forbearance on the present. There was nothing that could have prepared me for the onslaught of memory, thoughts, emotions, expectations, and hope that accompanies a Cern into the conscience of a sentient being. It was being two people at once. I retained my identity as Casey Winsum, but I also became Jenna. I guess the best way to describe it is to say that it was as though I was Jenna having an out-of-body experience. I could observe everything about her from both within and without, but in no way could I initiate her thoughts and actions. I was a passenger privy to her entire being, and I was convinced that I was, in fact, both Jenna Henson and Casey Winsum.

* * *

The alarm on my new-fangled smart-phone was playing Reveille, and I reluctantly gave up the ridiculous dream I'd been having. I slapped at the phone until it went quiet and groaned loudly. I shouldn't have drank so much last night! Becca and Jennifer had drug me to that Back-To-School party last night, and we'd ended up playing beer pong. It seemed every inch of my body ached, even my breasts. I groaned again when I realized I hadn't taken my contacts out before passing out in my bed last night. My eyes were dry and cloudy. I sat up and rubbed them gently trying to generate some tears. I so wanted to lie back down and sleep off the rest of this hangover! After several minutes and about a hundred blinks, my vision cleared, and the clock now said 6:07. Do I really want to be a lawyer? But tuition had been paid, and today was the first day of grad school. I had Intro to Law at 8:00, and it was a 45 minute drive to campus.

Tentatively, I stood and waited a moment to be sure my balance was right. I glanced at the mirror on the door of my bedroom. My hair was a hot mess from the top of my head to the middle of my back. Damn! I need to cut that shit off! I pulled my nighty over my head and shuffled into the bathroom, turned on the shower, and sat down to pee. With elbows on my knees, I rested my head in my hands and closed my eyes. A measure of relief came as I emptied my over-filled bladder. The shower was starting to steam. Still lethargic, I pulled a length of toilet paper, folded it, and wiped myself. Oh great. My period was starting! No wonder I feel like crap!

I stepped into the shower and just stood there for several minutes relishing the heat and massage of the spraying water. At length, I squeezed some shampoo into a palm and began rubbing it into my hair. The roots cried out in pain, and I groaned again. I rinsed my hair and soaped myself with body wash. If Mom knew how much I liked to touch myself and be touched, she'd insist I schedule a long session with Reverend O'Reilly. But here, in the shower, I took pleasure while thoroughly scrubbing my body.

By the time I'd toweled off and blew my hair dry, I was starting to feel a bit more normal. I wriggled into a sports bra, inserted a tampon, and selected some lacey panties from my dresser. So. What do I wear on the first day of law school? I wasn't feeling very gregarious, so I went with plain, unattractive attire. Old blue jeans, a t-shirt that was too large to define my breasts, and a pair of tiny faux diamond earrings was as much as I wanted. I pulled on mid-calf socks and laced up some running shoes halfway. I bunched my hair into a pony tail and then curled it into a ball which I fastened at the back with a straight metal clasp. I looked in the mirror again and decided I looked a little too much like a boy. Fine. I'll put on just a little make-up, but I didn't want to be having guys hitting on me all day. I just wasn't in the mood!

I was in the kitchen, a cup of coffee was brewing, and I'd found a package of strawberry Pop Tarts that would do for breakfast when my phone rang. It was nearly 7:00.

"Hi, Mom." I put the phone on speaker while I finished making my cup of coffee.

"Are you on campus yet?" asked my mother with excitement.

"Almost!" I lied, "Sitting in a bit of traffic at the moment."

"I am so proud of you, Jenna! You're going to be the first lawyer in the family! The Lord has blessed you with a fine mind, and I know you will breeze through it all, just as you did your bachelor's".

"I'm grateful to have your confidence, Mom."

"Oh, Jenna, don't be silly! You know I'm your number one fan! Just you and me, right, kiddo?" I hated when she called me kiddo. She started that after Dad left us. Kiddo was his pet name for me!

"Sure, Mom. I'll do my best to make you proud. Oh, look! The traffic is starting to move! I better get off here. I hate talking on the phone while driving."

"I know, kiddo. I just wanted to remind you that the prayer meeting Wednesday night will be at the Mulholland's. You'll still be able to make it won't you?"

"I don't know. Probably. I'll let you know. I gotta go now!"

"Of course, have a good first day at LAW SCHOOL!! Yay!!!" Thank God she hung up! I loved my mother dearly, but she could really get under my skin with her ever-present positivity and religious expectations.

The drive into the city wasn't nearly as bad as I'd pretended. I managed to find the classroom fairly easily and slipped into a seat near the top of the lecture hall at 7:58. It was a large room, nearly an auditorium that seated perhaps 200 students. Most of the rows below me were chock full of people. Chattering and the sound of cell phones beeping, pinging, and ringing filled the air. In the lecture pit stood a podium equipped with a microphone. A half-dozen speakers were mounted on either side of the hall. It took me a couple minutes of fumbling to set my phone to record the lecture. Just as I figured it out, the room began to quiet quickly. A young man had stepped up to the microphone. I was immediately attracted to his lean build, bright eyes, dark hair, and wide smile.

"Good morning, ladies and gentlemen! Welcome to Introduction to law. I'm Mr. Winsum, one of Professor Gingrich's TA's, and I'll be one of your instructors this semester. How many of you noticed today that Pfizer settled the largest health care fraud case in history to the tune of $2.3 billion?"

Everyone started looking around at each other, but no one raised their hand. After several seconds, Mr. Winsum said "Ignorance of the law is no excuse, people." Several students laughed, and he flashed a wide smile to the room. "I'll expect you to stay current on major legal cases from now on. We'll be discussing fundamental principles of law that each case brings to our attention. In the case of Pfizer, one of the first and most fundamental of all law principles came into play."

He continued with his lecture, but I was experiencing a growing appreciation of this man. His voice was smooth and clear, conveying both intelligence and affability. He constantly panned the audience as he spoke, and I could swear he looked directly at me several times during the fifty minute lecture. His bright blue eyes were worthy of worship, and there was something about the way he moved while he talked that made me tingle, just a bit. It was a good thing I was recording the lecture, because my attention was divided between what he said and how he said it. I found myself fantasizing intimate encounters with him. I definitely had to meet this guy!

After completing his lecture, Mr. Winsum made an announcement. "One last thing. Professor Gingrich will be hosting a meet-and-greet for all first year law students this afternoon at 4:00 in the Bliley Commons. There will be refreshments and even some entertainment! I hope to see many of you there." Was he looking right at me again?

I had two more classes that morning and another at 3:00 that afternoon. During each of them, I found it difficult to concentrate. I was trying to think of some way, some excuse to speak with Mr. Winsum during the afternoon soiree. One minute I was fantasizing about him and the next admonishing myself for even considering it. Despite assurances from Becca and Jennifer as well as my mother that I was indeed an attractive and worthy woman, and even given the attempts from many boys throughout high school and college that tried to date me, I'd never been alone with a man. I was terrified of rejection. I feared any relationship I might develop would end up with them just picking up and leaving one day, just like Dad did. His last words to me still rang loudly in my ears. "I don't even know why I tried, kiddo. I guess I never really wanted a family." I'd adored him, loved him, and trusted him, but he'd left me standing there in the living room with tears running down my eight-year-old face. He'd walked out the door without another word, and I hadn't seen nor heard from him since. For all I knew, he could be dead by now.

My 3:00 class ran over by a few minutes, and by the time I hustled over to the Commons, there were several dozen people milling around, holding paper cups of punch, and talking quietly in groups at small tables. I found Becca at a large table that held several platters of various finger foods. My stomach was still a bit unsettled due to the hangover, but I'd skipped lunch, and even the generic little ham sliders were looking pretty appetizing. "They any good?" I asked Becca.

"Not as delicious as he is!" she pointed across the room. Becca was always angling to hook up with some guy, only to have a different one by next Tuesday. I wasn't sure why she had commitment issues, but it was something we shared without discussing.

"Gezzy weezy, Becca! Is sex the only thing you think about?" I hadn't looked where she'd pointed. Instead, I chose a plate, grabbed some food from four different platters, and dipped out a cup of punch. We walked to one of the vacant small tables that had been set up for seating and eating. We settled down, and I took a bite of a slider. Oh, yes! Food was what I wanted right then! I gobbled three of them and washed them down with half the cup of punch.

"So, how was your first day of law school?" asked Becca.

"It would have been a lot better without having played beer pong last night. I'm just now starting to feel normal." I spoke while chewing yet another slider, "You get one of those roast beefs? They're pretty good!"

"Naw," said Becca, chewing on a celery stick, "if I ate like you, I'd be giving the Goodyear Blimp a run for its money. How you don't get fat with all you eat I'll never figure out. Besides, I need to stay in shape, if I ever hope to get a man like that!" She subtly pointed across the room again, but I was more interested in protein than eye candy – I'd had a whole bag full of candy during Intro to Law. I'd made a point of not scanning the room when I entered. I was still debating whether or not to engage Mr. Winsum should the opportunity arise. Every time I thought of him, my breath came a tad quicker.

"Oh shit!" exclaimed Becca, "He's coming this way!" She began a series of discreet primping moves to her hair and clothing.

"Don't make a spectacle of yourself, Becca. Do you always have to be in heat?" I was still concentrating on my meal and feeling better each time I swallowed.

"Good afternoon, ladies! I trust you are enjoying yourselves!" I hadn't seen him approach, but I recognized his voice immediately. That smooth, melodic tenor could only be Mr. Winsum! I literally choked a bit, and a small morsel of roast beef flew onto the paper tablecloth.

"It would be more enjoyable if you'd join us for a few minutes." lured Becca, batting her eyes twice accompanied by a suggestive smile.

"The pleasure would be all mine," said Mr. Winsum, "but I've got a lot of students to meet today, so I'll just introduce myself, exchange some pleasantries, and move on. My name is Casey Winsum. I teach Intro to Law."

By then, it would have been rude not to look at him. When I did, I felt my heart skip a beat! This man was even more gorgeous up close! My eyes opened wide, and I couldn't help but to smile brightly.

"I'm Becca Faraday," responded Becca, holding out her hand. "I was in your class this morning. Front row!" He grasped her hand lightly and said, "I'm very pleased to meet you, Becca!" He turned to me and said, "And you are…".

Good lord! What was my name? "J-Jenna!" I stammered, "Jenna Henson." He held his hand out to me as a greeting. I'd become so flustered at his sudden appearance that I'd hesitated to offer mine. I quickly did with a bit too much intent and shook his hand like a man. Becca snickered under her breath, and I shot her a disciplinary glance. My face flushed a shade red.

A dozen things ran through my mind, but before I could choose something else to say, he said, "Jenna. What a lovely name! You were sitting in the top row this morning, weren't you?"

He'd noticed me!! His cobalt blue eyes were locked on mine. They were warm and congenial, his smile easy and natural. "Yes!" I finally managed, "You must have eyes like an eagle!"

He laughed. "I doubt that. Sometimes I can't find my butt with both hands!" I bet I could find it was my immediate thought. It took everything I had not to look at it. Instead, and to my chagrin, I giggled like a pre-teen. Becca snickered again, more obviously. I could feel my face grow hot with a deeper blush of red. Casey's smile grew more amused, but not in a mocking way. He changed the subject, "Listen, Jenna, I'm organizing a study group – all the TA's do – and I was wondering if you'd like to join mine. They are groups of six, and I like to meet on Wednesday evenings from 6 till 10. What do you say?"

His expression was as inviting as the rest of his body. I struggled not to answer too quickly then blurted out, "Sure! Why not?!"

"Great! We meet in one of the study alcoves at the law library, number 16. I'll be looking forward to you joining us. It's been a pleasure to meet you!" He shook my hand again, turned to Becca, bowed ever so slightly, smiled and said, "Ms. Faraday. Have a good day!" And then he was off to another group.

"Well, I'll be damned!" said Becca. "He was ALL over you! Barely even looked at me! I think he likes you!" She broke out in a sing-song, "Jenna and Casey sittin' in a tree.."

"Oh, shut up, Becca! It's just a study group!"

"Uh huh, I saw what you were studying! Don't you think it's about time you started sampling what you want so much?"

"What I want is a law degree. I don't have time for…" my brow furrowed, "complications."

* * *

That's when the Cern dissolved and I was once again myself, in the classroom, holding hands with Jenna. I blinked several times, dumbfounded, speechless, and completely entranced with what I'd just experienced. Jenna looked exhausted. Her face was hectic and embarrassed. Tears streamed down her face. Yet, her hands gripped mine like vices. Her countenance was puzzling.

On the other hand, I was utterly ecstatic! "Holy Mother of God!" I finally blurted, "I was you! I was a woman! That was incredible!" I had become Jenna, as privy to her thoughts, emotions, and body as I was to my own. It was as different as watching a rollercoaster is to riding one. Being someone else was the epitome of empathy, and my soul was begging for more. But, as much as I wanted to jump back in, I couldn't ignore the state of malaise displayed by Jenna. "Do you want to take a break?" I asked tentatively.

Jenna rolled her eyes and sniffed up some snot. She shook her head hard in response to my question, grimaced with determination and invoked the Cern once again.

* * *

"It's not much, but its mine!" I said as I unlocked the door to my bungalow. Casey was behind me, one strap of his backpack slung over his shoulder. We had ten days until the second semester started, and I'd invited Casey to spend it with me. I'd finished semester exams on Wednesday, gone to the eye doctor to get new contacts on Thursday morning, completed my six-month check-up with my doctor Thursday afternoon and stocked up with enough food for the week ahead with an evening run to Whole Foods. I didn't want any chores nagging for my attention during this vacation.

"C'mon in! Make yourself at home!" My tone was light, but I was feeling anything but carefree. For me, I was taking a huge risk allowing him to cohabitate with me. I was about to bare much more of myself than just my body, and I was terrified I was making a huge mistake. The past five months had been crazy, fun, scary, and amazing. After our third study session, Casey had asked me if I'd like to grab a cup of coffee. I'd broken my own rule, and with immense trepidation said, "Sure!" We'd sat in that all-night diner talking until one in the morning. We talked about the law, the school, Professor Gingrich, the inauguration of our first black President, the rising price of gas, and, of course, the weather. Though mid-February, it had been unseasonably warm, even for Tampa.

Casey had been so easy to talk to. He made me laugh often with his feigned cluelessness or his elaborate references to silly laws that never existed. I'd been as nervous as a porcupine in a balloon factory that first date, but he'd done and said everything necessary to put me at ease. By the end of that first night, it was clear to me that I was going to be willing to do exactly what Becca had suggested: I was going to sample the goods, at last.

"I have frosted mugs in the freezer! You want a root beer?" I asked temptingly. Early in our relationship, we'd discovered that we both preferred sugary drinks instead of coffee or alcohol most of the time.

"That would be almost as perfect as you!" replied Casey. I was a sucker for his compliments, and he knew it. "I love your décor!"

I looked at him askance. "What décor? I'm hardly ever here except to sleep!" The walls were bare except for a few pictures on one living room wall. I didn't even have a TV. A sofa, a low table in front of it, a floor lamp, and an area rug were all the living room contained.

"Early 21st Century Minimalist!" Casey nodded in approval. "I like it. It suits you!"

Casey had a knack for painting everything with a bright brush. It was like salve for my constant worrying and the fear that always simmered below my professional veneer. He followed me into the kitchen. I took the mugs from the freezer and set them on the table.

"Aha! A dinette in a kitchenette. That seals the deal: definitely Minimalist!"

He came up behind me, wrapped his arms around my waist, and kissed me tenderly at the nape of my neck. Every time he touched me – no matter where – it sent vibrations through me that were irresistible. A small moan escaped me, but I pulled away and said, "Slow down, Romeo, we'll have ample opportunity to exercise our freedom over the next ten days!" The truth was that making love to Casey completely shattered my composure. It made me as pliable as silly putty and not much more intelligent than that. His touch unlocked the tight hold I'd maintained over my physical urges since puberty. The first time we'd made love was epic for me, and I yearned for it each time we were together. Worse, he knew that, and I couldn't help but consider at times that he was merely using me.

"Don't you dare go there, Jenna!" Casey said with feigned superiority. "Don't you ever think that this is all just a…" he made a goofy face, moved his arms and legs preposterously, and in a comedic voice continued, "fancy dance to get in your pants!"

I laughed at his rhyme and antics as I opened the fridge to get the Hires. I'd prayed so many times that this man was genuine, and I did so again. I came back with, "You'd look ridiculous in my panties!" We both shared a merry laugh.

After rehydrating, I took him for a long walk on the beach. We delighted in the salt air, the seagulls, and waved often at passing watercraft. A few even sounded their foghorns in salutation. At length we came upon a board walk. We found a food cart, ordered a couple Habana sandwiches, and found a small table at which to sit and enjoy our lunch.

"This is all wonderful, Jenna! Your little cottage, the uncrowded beach, quaint little food truck, and genuine Cuban food! It's a far cry from the plains of Iowa that I grew up on. Why have you been hiding this place from me?" asked Casey.

Because I'm afraid I'll let you in, and then you'll leave when you get tired of it! "I don't know." I lied. "Maybe I was keeping it as a surprise!" Did he notice my eyes were not smiling?

"It's a good surprise. I like it a lot!" He took another bite of his sandwich. He chewed and swallowed, then said "Not very many kids around here."

"Of course not. It's a normal Friday for public schools, silly. They're all in the cafeteria or P.E. right now."

He raised his eyebrows in faux surprise. "Hm…What an excellent point, Solicitor Henson. Still, it's a shame." He took another bite.

"Why?" I asked.

"Kid's are cool. Some of my favorite people have been – or are – kids." He was talking while chewing. "I plan on having a whole gang of them myself someday."

I was taken aback. "What?? The day after tomorrow?? What kids?"

Casey stopped chewing momentarily trying to figure out why I'd just said what I had. He swallowed and said more clearly, "Someday, not Sunday."

"Oh!" I snorted a laugh which made Casey giggle.

"You're beautiful when you're gay!" he managed between guffaws.

"Oh really? So now you think I'm gay?" I was still laughing myself.

Casey suddenly got serious. "No ma'am. I definitely don't think you are gay. In fact, I'm certain you are at least bi-sexual. Eyewitness evidence is incontrovertible!" He was pointing at his own eyes. Then he pointed at my boobs. We both broke into new gales of laughter.

I loved it when he played with me like that! He was practically a kid himself sometimes. It was so easy to be free with Casey! I wondered if I was falling in love. I found the notion both thrilling and terrifying.

Casey popped the last of his sandwich in his mouth, chewed some more and continued with "Seriously, though, Jenna. I want to have a bunch of kids." He swallowed, guzzled the last of his soda, and looked me in the eye waiting for a relevant response.

Did he just ask me to marry him? I shifted uncomfortably in my chair, momentarily at a loss for words. Six months ago, I was a virgin. Now, I was being asked to have a litter! I pretended to have not read between the lines. "Bananas come in bunches. What, you want quintuplets or something?"

"That'd be OK, too. Fine by me." He smiled affectionately, and I felt those irresistible vibrations down low. This man could fuck me with a grin. "I mean, someday, you know, after I get a job with some big-ass law firm and am pulling in a six-figure salary. Three girls and two boys, at least, all at once or one at a time, in any order. It don't matter."

"It doesn't matter." I corrected.

"Nope, it don't." he agreed, conclusively. With that, he stood up quickly and said with excitement "Hey! Why don't we see if we can rent some jet skis? Whadaya say?"

We made a quick trip back to my place to pick up swim wear and a fresh set of clothing for afterwards. We spent the afternoon buzzing the beaches of Old Tampa Bay and weaving in and out and around the massive pylons that supported the Frankland Bridge. That evening, Casey took me to see the debut of Friday The 13th after a delightful dinner of lobster, shrimp, and steak at a one of those Japanese places where the chef makes your dinner right in front of you Casey was charming and playful throughout, and by the time we got back to my bungalow shortly before midnight, we were both proclaiming that it had been the happiest day of our lives.

Being with Casey was magical! His easy way was never demanding and always accommodating. He made me feel so special. He hadn't said it yet, but I was certain he was falling in love with me. I wondered if what I felt for him was love. How could I know? I'd never been in love before, but I knew one thing. I never wanted him to leave!

"Ughh!" I exclaimed, "Those showers at the Skidoo place were so lame. I can still smell the saltwater in my hair! Do you mind if I take a quick shower? I don't want this crap all over my pillow."

"No! Yeah, sure, take your time. I'm kinda beat myself, and bed is sounding awfully good right now."

I smiled with surprise for there had been no hint of sexual innuendo in his voice. He was sitting on the couch and really did look tired, his eyelids drooped and his face was far less animated than usual, though still soft and kind. I liked my shower hot and steamy, and that night, it proved be as soporific as it was cleansing. By the time I shut the water off, I was so lethargic, I nearly tripped getting out of the tub. I found myself disappointed that Casey hadn't joined me in the shower, but thankful at the same time. I wrapped myself in just a towel and walked back into the living room. Casey was laid out on the couch asleep, snoring softly, just a hint of a smile remained on his lips. I cocked my head and smiled in surprise. It was as if he was giving me the freedom to do what I most wanted to do at that moment. I turned off the floor lamp, padded into the bedroom and was asleep before my head hit the pillow.

Saturday morning dawned with bright skies and low humidity. When I finally opened my eyes, it was past 9:30. As the fog of sleep receded from my brain, I noticed the smell of bacon and was unnerved to find that it nauseated me, just a little. I got out of bed, pulled on a thin robe and walked into the kitchen. My dear Casey was standing at the stove, an apron hung around his neck, pouring pancake batter into a hot skillet.

"Ah! Perfect timing! Breakfast is nearly ready!" Casey was exuberant and back to his lively self. He handed me a glass of milk and said, "Have a seat m'lady. Breakfast will be served momentarily." He turned back to the stove, flipped the pancake, took some buttermilk biscuits from the oven, and loaded two on each plate that already contained several strips of bacon and a couple or three pancakes. Sausage gravy, butter, syrup, and utensils were already on the table. He shoveled the last pancake onto the plate that only had two and served them both to the table. "Voila!" he said with a flourish. He removed his apron, sat down, and said in a surprisingly accurate Humphrey Bogart impression, "Dig in, Schweetheart. Eat hearty! We have a glorioush day ahead of ush!"

I was laughing and shaking my head, "You're incorrigible! I didn't know you knew how to cook!"

His voice assumed that of a haughty chef. "Madam, I have fried bacon for the finest European royalty!" He continued as plain, old, affable Casey, "Besides, I was raised with a couple hundred of the finest hogs in Iowa. More than a few ended up just like that." He pointed at the bacon on my plate.

The bacon was cooked crispy, just the way I liked it, but when I looked down at it, a bit of bile rose in my throat. I made a sickly face and swallowed hard, looking away.

Casey noticed, and alarm overtook his countenance, "What's wrong? I thought you loved bacon."

I took three swallows of milk, and the nausea subsided. I managed a smile and said "Nothing. Nothing at all. Everything is just perfect!"

Casey was unconvinced. "Are you sure? You looked like I just sat a plate of worms in front of you." Concern still furrowed his brow.

I buttered my cakes, poured on some syrup, sliced off a thick triangle, and shoved it in my mouth. "Mmmmm! Oh, Casey, these are wonderful! Banana! My favorite!" I beamed at him appreciatively as I chewed, privately wondering if I'd gag when I tried to swallow. I didn't, though. Instead, my appetite came roaring back, and I became single-minded in the pursuit of making myself a hog. After several bites of everything, I finally glanced over at Casey. He'd stopped eating himself and was just sitting there with amusement, like a spectator. "Don't even think about butchering me!" I declared. He howled with laughter. I couldn't stop a half smile as I shot him a glance of mock annoyance and just kept on eating.

If Friday had been the happiest day of our lives, Saturday proved to be even better. Casey took me to Busch Gardens! We rode nearly every ride, ate junk food, and he even won me a huge stuffed pelican by throwing rings onto Coca Cola bottles. He rarely let go of my hand, often had his arm around me, and we made out erotically when stopped at the top of the Ferris wheel. At nightfall, we snuggled together on a wooden bench to watch the fireworks display. The show was building to the finale, multiple rockets bursting in the air. I leaned close to Casey's ear and whispered, "That's how I feel when we make love."

Casey glance at me quickly with surprise and wonderment, and just then the cherry bombs started going off. They were so powerful that we could feel the concussions. Casey turned to me and yelled "That's how I feel when we make love!"

We got back to my bungalow a little after 11:00 and wasted no time in beginning our own fireworks show. Casey enjoyed touching me as much as I enjoyed being touched, and he took his sweet time about it, too. He kissed and caressed and squeezed and licked me in all the right places until I was wet and begging for him to enter, but he only redoubled his efforts to bring me to the brink of orgasm before he even opened his condom. He was always gentle and unhurried, and never failed to find some new way to excite me beyond tolerance. Outside the bedroom, Casey was playful and childlike, but while making love, he was resolute in his efforts to pleasure me with soft strokes, strong hugs, and sweet nothings whispered in my ear. By the time he finally slipped on the condom and entered me, the sensation shattered my reality, and all that existed was his soul massaging mine. Once he was inside me, I climaxed quickly and powerfully, but he'd just keep pumping, driving me to ever higher plateaus of sensation and several more orgasms. My pleasure seemed to supply his pleasure. I was breathless with vibration, covered with sweat, and begging him to finish before he finally let go and exploded himself with strong, deep spasms of his own.

He rolled off of me, and we remained silent as we waited for our breathing to return to normal. He was still holding my hand, ever reluctant to leave me all alone. I was watching the ceiling fan spin lazily, enjoying the evaporation of perspiration. Dare I say it? Shall I set the stage for abandonment? I couldn't imagine living a day without him by my side. "I've fallen in love with you, Casey Winsum."

He rolled sideways to face me propping his head on his hand. He looked at me with a broad smile and said, "What a coincidence! I've fallen in love with you, too!"

Could it be true? Did he really love me? My heart was pounding out of my chest. Tears of both terror and joy filled my eyes. I searched his face for any sign of deception, but all I saw was the same warmth that was always there for me, that I had feared he might show some other woman, but had failed to ever observe. I pulled him to me and hugged him wordlessly, willing my soul to fuse with his. He responded in kind and held me with a delicate strength. In that moment, I felt secure for the first time since I was a small child.

Sunday morning we rented bicycles and toured the beaches of St. Petersburg along Gulf Boulevard. We stopped for lunch at Dockside Dave's, then played three games of miniature golf at Smuggler's Cove. We laughed, played, and competed with a natural ease like school children during an endless recess.

As the week flew by, we made love nightly and filled our days with museums, concerts, shopping, art galleries, bowling, and even went deep sea fishing on Friday. I hooked a decent sized marlin, and Casey helped me battle the poor creature onto the boat for over 90 minutes. Was there anything this man wouldn't or couldn't do for me?

We were both exhausted by the time we returned to my bungalow that evening. Our shoulders ached from wrestling that marlin! I called up some quiet jazz on my iPhone and piped it through a modest sound bar I'd picked up at Best Buy on one of our shopping sprees. We spent a long time massaging mango-scented lotion into each other's bodies and talked quietly of our mutual love and exclusive commitment to one another.

Casey mentioned often that week how beautiful our children would be, but always added that he was in no rush. In fact, he was rather adamant about us both completing our degrees and landing good jobs before starting a family. We mused about marriage and debated the merits and disadvantages of a large wedding, though we spoke speculatively and without a timeline.

Saturday morning, I woke to tired muscles and more than slight nausea, which I chalked up to the spicy Mexican food we'd ordered for delivery the previous evening, not to mention all the junk food I'd carelessly consumed all week. Casey was appropriately concerned. He suggested we take a break and stay home for the day. I privately leaped for joy when he called my bungalow 'home'. We ended up exercising only our brains that day, playing lazy games of Trivial Pursuit, Scrabble, and several games of chess. We were so evenly matched in so many ways that it was even pleasurable whenever one of us lost.

We slept in late on Sunday and settled for a long stroll through the Florida Botanical Gardens in the afternoon. That evening we built a fire on the beach behind my bungalow, roasted weenies on sticks, and made S'Mores. We lay on a blanket and explored the Milky Way, pointing out our favorite constellations to each other amid frequent laughter, abundant kisses and affectionate caresses. The moon was as golden as honey, as full as our love for each other, and as bright as our future. We finished our evening with a magical, glorious, and joyful physical union.

I awoke early Monday morning, before Casey, with some nagging nausea again. I slipped out of bed quietly, pulled on my robe, slipped into my bunny slippers, picked up my phone, turned off its alarm, and padded to the kitchen to find something to settle my stomach. I toasted a couple pieces of bread, poured a glass of milk, and carried my meager breakfast to the living room. I settled on the couch and checked my phone for any messages. Second semester classes began at 10:00, but it was not quite 8:00 yet. I'd only opened Messenger when the incoming call chime went off. I swallowed the bite of toast in my mouth with a bit of a gag, swiped to accept the call, and said, "Hello?"

"Jenna Henson?" asked a polite and cheerful female voice.

"Yes, this is she."

"This is Elsie from Dr. Shaziri's office. We had a little snafu with your blood work, and I'm sorry it took so long to get back to you, but – um – well, Congratulations! You're pregnant!"

Terror ripped through my body! I dropped the toast still in my right hand. My voice was hoarse, and I could only whisper a strangled "What??!!"

"Yep!" said Elsie cheerfully, "No doubt about it! Dr. Shaziri wants you to see Dr. Brooker at Northside hospital right away. There were a few anomalies in your blood work – nothing to be concerned about – but they should be addressed ASAP. I took the liberty of scheduling you an appointment with Dr. Brooker, an excellent obstetrician, this morning at 10 A.M., I hope that works for you."

My heart was pounding like a jackhammer, my skin – crawling and clammy! I felt like I couldn't breathe, but could drop dead right then and there. This cannot be happening!! Casey always used protection! Our classes started in a couple of hours. We had degrees to complete. There was no time for a baby. And I was wholly unprepared to be a mother! And Casey! He would be furious! He'd been steadfast in his determination to wait for a family! I had to stop this before he found out!

I gathered myself enough to say, "Ahhh….yeah, yeah. I can do that."

"Great!" said Elsie, "I'll call and confirm the appointment for you! Again, congratulations! And good luck! Don't celebrate too much!" she warned and ended the call.

Holy fuck! Oh shit! I quickly slipped back into the bedroom and got dressed as quietly as I could. Casey was still sound asleep, but I knew he'd set his alarm for 8:15. I flew out the door five minutes before it would wake him and began the drive to the hospital complex.

I drove mindlessly as my brain was laser-focused on the crisis at hand. I could not lose the love of my life! This thing in my belly would ruin it all! I replayed in my mind every time we'd had sex, and I was certain Casey had always used a condom. How in the hell could this have happened? Then I thought of my mother. She was a devout Baptist and would be utterly devastated if I had a child out of wedlock. I'd never hear the end of it! She often referred to a 'bastard' cousin I had. This had to stop, and it had to stop today!

When I got to the hospital complex, I had to Google Dr. Brooker to find his office. My phone had been going off repeatedly, Casey trying to call me. I'd ignored them all, and after locating the doctor's office, turned off my phone. By the time I walked up to the intake desk, it was exactly 10:00, and I was breathless from hurry.

"Jenna Henson for Dr. Brooker. I have a 10:00 appointment!" I gushed to the receptionist.

"Yes! We were expecting you! Have a seat, and we'll be right with you."

The waiting room walls were adorned with pictures of happy babies, radiant mothers, and proud fathers. I groaned as a fresh and strong wave of nausea flushed through me. It was only a moment before a nurse opened a door and called my name. She led me down a corridor to an open door that proved to be Dr. Brooker's office. He was seated behind a modest desk, reviewing something on his computer monitor. "Dr. Brooker, Jenna Henson." introduced the nurse.

Dr. Brooker looked to be north of 50, bald on top with salty brown fringe. He lifted his head toward me, but his eyes lingered a few more seconds on the screen before meeting mine. He smiled unenthusiastically and motioned for me to have a seat. He started right in, "I was just reviewing your labs that Dr. Shaziri sent over, Jenna. Will this be your first child?"

"Absolutely not! I don't want it!" I crossed my arms, scowling and studying the back of his monitor.

The doctor seemed unperturbed. "Do you know who the father is? Have you discussed this with him?"

My body language remained obstinate, and I restated my position more firmly, "I don't want it!"

Dr. Brooker took a moment to absorb my determination. "I see. Well, then, since your hCG levels were quite strong – what was it? – eleven days ago, levonorgestrel is out of the question. Your only option is invasive abortion. It's a quick procedure, perhaps five or ten minutes, but some women find it unbearably uncomfortable, others not so much. Some don't feel anything more than tugging and a few twinges of pain. Do you tolerate pain well?" He simply wanted an answer.

Not really, I thought. "Can you give me something like when I had my wisdom teeth cut out?"

The doctor finally cracked half a smile and said, "Something like that, sure. A minimal IV drip of propofol would leave you with no memory of the procedure, though it will take perhaps an hour to fully recover, and you should have someone with you to drive you home. When would you like to schedule it?"

I looked at the doctor with disbelief. My voice rose with irritability, "Schedule? Oh no, we're going to do this today! I want it out, and I want it out now!" I must have appeared to be quite out of my mind. The doctor made a face as though he would object, then seemed to reconsider. He moved his mouse and clicked a few times, then pressed a button on an intercom. "Elsie, please reschedule the Redsetter follow-up for Wednesday, and ask Margaret to prep the procedure suite for an abortion at 11:30." He released the intercom button and continued to me, "Quick enough?" he smiled hopefully.

I finally relaxed a little and exclaimed, "Thank God! Ughhh! I want to get this over with!"

"Yeah. I noticed." Dr. Brooker actually winked at me.

I spent the next hour filling out medical history and insurance forms, answering pre-op questions, and finally, I changed into a gown just after 11:00. I had never been so single-minded in my life. My mission was to save my heart, my love, my life with Casey. I'd have let them cut off my right hand before I'd ever let Casey know I'd been pregnant.

Margaret had me lay on a gurney that folded down at the knees and was equipped with stirrups. She started an IV with a saline drip in a vein on the back of my left hand and rolled over a tray with several scary-looking instruments on it as well as a syringe of what I assumed to be propofol. She chattered lightly about the weather, but I was not in the mood to respond. Dr. Brooker came in at precisely 11:30, gowned and gloved. He reached the gurney before he looked at me and simply said, "Last chance to bail…."

"Do it, Doc. Just do it!"

He nodded at me, then glanced at Margaret with a go ahead look. She picked up the syringe and slowly injected it into the IV port. I fell asleep in just seconds.

"Jenna?"

Who was calling my name? My eyes fluttered and finally opened. I was still on the gurney, but in a different room. It was cool and smelled sterile. My head and shoulders were propped up and cushioned by a generous pillow. The first thing that came into focus was the large analog clock on the wall. It read 1:12. Margaret was beside me, holding a paper cup.

"Would you like some ginger ale?"

My wits returned quickly. I took the cup from Margaret, but before sipping, I asked, "Did he get it out?"

Margaret smiled sympathetically and said "Of course he did. Drink up! Dr. Brooker will be in shortly to speak with you." She left the room.

The ginger ale was wonderfully refreshing. I finished it rather quickly and wished for more. Footsteps approached in the corridor, and Dr. Brooker walked in. He asked, "Are you feeling any pain?"

I wriggled my pelvis a little, but felt nothing but a sense of violation. I planted my feet to push myself up a little on the gurney and a brief, but sharp pang shot through my abdomen. "Uh, yeah! There's a little! It's not too bad."

"Good! Margaret will give you some Vicodin that should handle any residual pain. You might be sore for a day or two." He was writing on a clipboard as he spoke. "Took a little longer than I expected." His tone was matter of fact. He finished writing and finally looked at me. His countenance gave me pause, but it was indecipherable. The doctor read my concern and assured me that "The procedure was successful, you're no longer pregnant."

There was clearly something he wasn't telling me. "Why," I asked, "did it take longer than expected?"

"I had to take several samples to send for analysis We'll know for sure by tomorrow afternoon," his eyes got sad, "but I've seen it often enough. It is unusual in someone as young as you. Frankly, I'm surprised you even got pregnant."

Terror-fueled adrenaline shot through my body. What was he saying? Analysis? Unusual?? Cancer?? Oh, God, no!

That bastard let me marinate in fear for several seconds before he said, "Endometriosis. All over the place down there. When confirmed, and as widespread as it seems to be, hysterectomy is indicated." He continued on for several minutes, but I was too stunned to comprehend, his voice faded like frost in a microwave.

My mother had had a hysterectomy just three years ago. I knew what it meant: no children! I was devastated, holding on only to the slimmest chance that the doctor might be wrong. I went through the remainder of the visit like a robot, my emotions locked away until I could get away. I told them I'd order an Uber to get home, but once out of the office, I found my own car, drove to a cheap motel in West Tampa, and rented a room. My life was falling apart, and I needed to be alone.

I locked the motel room door, closed the blackout curtains, switched on a night stand lamp, stripped naked, and shuffled into the bathroom. There was no tub, but a roomy shower with an adjustable head that I set to massage. I started the water, and while it heated, I took two Vicodin and used the toilet.

I directed the steamy, pulsating spray so I could lay on the floor of the shower while it massaged my sore abdomen. Just twelve hours ago, I'd been so blissfully happy, and now I could barely believe what had happened in the meantime. I'd been so scared that Casey would leave me if he found out I was pregnant, and, in my single-minded determination that had served me so well throughout my pursuit of a college degree, had felt secure that I could make that problem go away with efficiency and posthaste. God, had that ever backfired! Sure, the pregnancy had been terminated, but now I was facing a barren future. It would break Casey's heart, and I was certain he'd discard me like a worn out battery. He'd find someone else to supply the gang of children he had planned for his family. He'd abandon me, just as my father had, but, ironically, for the exact opposite reason. My copious tears were lost in the shower water, and like my life, swirled down the drain.

I lay there until the water turned frigid, and I began to shiver. I dragged myself to my feet, turned off the water, and dried myself with a scratchy, white motel towel. I crawled under the covers of the bed, switched off the lamp, curled into a fetal position, and fell into an exhausted sleep, the faint hope that the doctor was wrong keeping me from completely losing my mind.

I dreamed I was back in high school. Billy Boster was my lab partner in chemistry. He was trying to convince me that he could make me want to have sex with him by mixing the chemicals set out before us. I was terrified he'd be successful and begged him not to do it. He was leering at me and telling me in evil, sultry tones that I wanted it, and he knew it. He poured one chemical, then another into a large flask. He set it upon a Bunsen Burner and turned up the flame. The mixture began to boil. He ignored my pleas to stop. He reached into a paper bag and pulled out a small, bloody mass of tissue. "All it needs now is a fetus!" his eyes were maniacal. He dropped the lump into the flask, and it exploded, fire erupted throughout the room. I screamed in terror and frantically searched the room for an exit. There were no doors. Billy was gone, and I was choking on thick smoke! I need to be rescued! At last I found the fire alarm on the wall and fought through the flames to reach it. I was coughing uncontrollably and had barely enough strength to pull the handle down. When the alarm began to blare, I awoke with a start, my heart pounding. A car alarm was blaring outside my room.

I groaned loudly, and by the time my breathing slowed, the alarm abruptly stopped. The room was pitch black, I could hear a TV faintly from the room next to mine. I fumbled to find the lamp and turned it on. The sudden light was painful, and I squeezed my eyes shut, then slowly blinked back to clear vision. My head pounded with ache, and my belly was throbbing with a dull discomfort. I got up, found the Vicodin, and washed down two with water, which tasted horrible. I realized I must be dehydrated, and despite my circumstances, I was really hungry!

I fished my phone from my purse and turned it on. It was nearly 11:00 P.M. I saw that Casey had called over two dozen times, and there were as many text messages from he, my mother, and Becca. I didn't want to read them, I didn't dial up my voicemail. Instead, I ordered a cheese pizza and a two-liter bottle of root beer from Pizza Hut for delivery. I turned my phone back off and left it on the nightstand. I didn't bother with underwear, but put on my shirt and pants. I didn't want to give the delivery guy anything to remember.

As I waited for the pizza, I began convincing myself that the doctor was wrong. I was only 22 years old! How the hell could I have endometriosis? That was a disease that I always thought was the misfortune of women who were near or beyond menopause. At that stage of life, a hysterectomy was merely discarding useless equipment, a cheat to lose a pound or two. That couldn't be happening to me! Over the past week, I'd imagined frequently what it would be like to have Casey's children. I'd grown accustomed to the thought and had held at bay that primal urge to reproduce. By the time the pizza showed up, I'd convinced myself that when I called the doctor tomorrow, he'd have to eat his words.

Tuesday morning proved rainy, cool, and dreary. Reruns of Criminal Minds had kept me up until 3:00 A.M., and it was now nearly noon. The pain in my belly was nearly gone, but I popped a couple more Vicodin, because I could. I turned my phone on to see if the doctor had called. Not yet, but there were many more calls from Casey and my mother. I turned the phone back off, got dressed, and went in search of an ice machine. Half the root beer remained and my throat felt parched. I blamed the medication.

The ice machine was flanked by several vending machines. I purchased several packages of junk and two additional bottles of Coke, filled a plastic bucket from the room with ice, and returned to my quarters. While woofing down a honey bun and six powdered donuts, I turned on my phone again. The doctor had called! I tapped the call back icon and waited for my call to be answered.

"Dr. Brooker's Office, how may I help you?" I recognized Elsie's voice.

"Jenna Henson returning Dr. Brooker's call."

"Oh, yes! Hold please."

Sweat broke out on my brow, my heartbeat quickened as did my breathing. This was taking too long! With the phone at my ear, I walked to the window and peeked out the drapes. A flash of lighting struck something not far from the motel, and a huge clap of thunder made me jump. It was pouring, the rain making foam in puddles. After several minutes, the doctor finally came on the line.

"Ms. Henson?" his voice was cool and clinical.

"Yes."

"Well, I got the results back from the lab. The endometriosis is widespread, and they also identified some pre-cancer cells. We'll need to schedule the hysterectomy at your earliest convenience. I can get it done for you next Tuesday morning if that works for you." Thunder cracked loudly outside the room.

I felt like I was about to pass out. This could not be happening! Tears streamed down my face. My hand holding the phone dropped to my side, and I dropped to my knees and screamed "Noooo!!!!"

I sobbed uncontrollably, alone in that dismal motel room. My life was ruined. Casey would surely hate me! Without him, life was not worth living! Eventually, a morbid quiet overtook my opiated mind. I struggled back to my feet, opened the motel door and walked out into the pouring rain. I simply didn't care anymore. Not about me, not about Casey, not about life. I walked through the thunderstorm, numb to the world, deep in despair.

The turbulent Old Tampa Bay was below me. Lightning still flashed, and thunder rolled. I raised my face to the heavens and God pummeled my face with rain. I stepped over the railing, looking down at the water churning below me. That ought to do it. My knees buckled, and the last complaint I had was that the fall took too long.

The Cern ended abruptly. Jenna released my hands, and we both staggered back into our respective chairs. She was exhausted and taking huge breaths, but was that relief on her face? As for myself, well, what could I say? I'd just lived the last twelve days of Jenna's life on Earth. I'd been her in every respect. I'd known her heart, her body, her every thought and memory. The mystery of her disappearance had been solved. At the time, I'd beaten myself up badly about it, thinking that I'd somehow scared her away or, worse, that she'd been kidnapped, tortured, raped, and murdered by some psychopathic serial killer. I'd buried the entire experience, locked it away in a part of my mind that had a door with a skull and crossbones on it. But the Cern had shattered that door and illuminated the truth! It had been an intoxicating and immensely satisfying experience. I didn't feel sad, after all, Jenna and Abby were still here, still loving me. I'd seen the universe and had Melted into much of it, but this Cern awoke within me an overwhelming craving to know every secret of every being everywhere. I wanted more!

Jenna had rested her head on the back of her chair, her eyes closed. The fingers of her right hand worried at a seam in the chair's upholstery, but she was otherwise still.

"Good God, Jenna!" I heaved a sigh. Her eyes opened, and she looked over at me with apprehension overlaid with hope.

Her anxiety melted when she saw the happiness, the love, the forgiveness that composed my expression. Her reservation toward me dissolved. Her instruction had been a success! She smiled contentedly and said, "Yes. Being God is good. Very good!" We both settled back in our chairs, reconsidering and relishing our mutual satisfaction.

After some moments I said, "So, were we really standing here holding hands for twelve days?"

Her laugh was light and quick. "No, Casey, Cerning is practically timeless, as quick as Melting." She rose from her chair, walked over to the buffet, and picked up a blueberry muffin. "Want one?" she asked.

"Sure, is there any root beer around here?" I ventured.

She reached into a refrigerated chest, pulled out two bottles of Hires, popped the caps, brought our mid-morning snack back to the table between our chairs, and sat back down. I took a big bite of the muffin and a long swallow of refreshment.

With a mouthful of muffin, I said, "You know, Jenna, I would have been perfectly happy to have adopted children with you, or even done without. I was completely smitten with you back then."

"I know." she admitted. "After my training here, I must have Cerned into you a million times. What I didn't know is how you'd react once you'd Cerned into me."

I nodded with an accepting smile, then looked at her quizzically. "But, you're God. If you are omniscient, you'd know everything, including how I'd react!"

She chuckled. "So typical of a newbie! We still have free will, even as God. The future is never certain; not a sure bet. All that stuff will be covered tomorrow. It's really quite interesting!"

I sighed. "Fine. So, what's next? As much as I enjoy being alone with you, it feels a little too lonely. Truth is, I would really like to Cern again! Being another being was captivating!"

Jenna nodded sincerely. "You don't have to tell me! Trust me. Cerning will be your entire reason for not destroying the whole universe. You'll never get enough of it. You'll pursue it and do it like a horny Bonobo!"

"A what?" I asked.

"They're monkeys. Bonobos are highly promiscuous, engaging in sexual interactions more frequently than any other primate, and in just about every combination from heterosexual to homosexual unions. Mothers even mate with their mature sons. Go ahead, cast a Melt and find some." she challenged.

I did, and she was right! "Wow! I think I knew some guys like that in college!" I laughed merrily. "But, c'mon Jenna, quit stalling! I want to Cern some more! Isn't that what you're supposed to be teaching me?"

"Alright! Alright already! Keep your shirt on! This next one is going to knock your sox off!" She was grinning wide and arched her eyebrows twice, quickly. "Cast a Melt, and find Arthur C. Fenstermeister in Springfield, Illinois. When you locate him, will a Cern, timeshift 48 hours."

"Timeshift? You mean 48 hours from now?" I asked

"Oh no!" Jenna said hurriedly, "God cannot see the future. We can only see what has been created, not what will be. You can timeshift as far back as you wish, but the future is never certain." She rolled her eyes. "We've been over this before, Casey. Tomorrow, you'll learn more about all that stuff. It's a paradox..." she sighed, "never mind, I'm straying from the lesson plan. Now, stop asking so many questions and complete the Cern."

I conjured the cast, found the man, and lived his life for 48 hours, all within a second or two. When the Cern dissolved, Jenna was looking at me with excited expectation. "Well? Did you like it?"

I was still entranced by what I'd just experienced. It took me a moment to focus back on Jenna. "No." I feigned disapproval. "I fucking loved it!!" I exclaimed.

"I knew you would!" squealed Jenna, jumping up from her chair, dancing from one foot to the other with pride and joy. She grabbed me by the shoulders. "Tell me! What was it like for you?"

"I don't know where to begin! It was like I had no soul, no heart, no empathy at all, not even for myself! I was pure evil! What I did to that woman, and...and those two little children!" I sucked in a breath as I heard their screams echoing in my mind.

"Yes!" urged Jenna "Go on!"

"I was an animal, a predator. I was driven by a singular need to cause pain and suffering – and I enjoyed it!! And, oh! Was I ever cunning and so capable of seeming to be quite the opposite of what I was. I was a master at manipulating people to gain their confidence, and then I'd strike like a rattlesnake! The terror in their eyes when they realized what I really was – was so, so satisfying! My sadism was like an aphrodisiac. The louder they screamed, the more they begged for their lives, the more aroused I became! When I finally swung that sledge hammer, driving that barbecue skewer through her right ear and out the left, I literally had an orgasm!"

"Yes! I'd never seen Fenny use a barbecue skewer before! That was intense!" Jenna was as excited as I was. She had Cerned into Fenny along with me!

I looked at Jenna with a new appreciation. We'd just shared a Cern into a being that was nothing like anything I'd ever considered. Sure, I'd defended some serial killers, without much luck. I'd noted their detachment, cold-heartedness, and some even had a charming and disarming charisma. But to actually be them, to know their mind, their motive, their inhuman lust for the agony of others was new, so novel, so fascinating, so pleasurable! To be someone so unlike oneself was utterly riveting!

"Intense doesn't begin to describe it, Jenna!" My tone became forceful, "I want to do another - someone different!"

Jenna beamed broadly, "I know!" she got wide-eyed and conspiratorial, "Let's go back and be the woman he killed, Darlene!"

We Cerned and returned as spontaneously and as quickly as a hiccup. My eyes were huge, my mouth agape. Jenna was holding her breath studying me with intense anticipation. I'd just suffered the horror of watching my children, Justin and Celine, being diced with a chainsaw. I'd gone insane with grief and terror. I'd endured more physical pain than I knew possible. I'd whimpered and begged and screamed until despair had numbed my soul. I'd looked a demon in the face and known helplessness. I'd prayed to God to rescue me, but instead my head became a shish kabob. "That was so…." I began.

"Gratifying?" ventured Jenna.

I looked at her with a touch of alarm. Her suggestion was too close for comfort. "Isn't it a bit wicked to take pleasure in the misfortune of others? What do the Germans call it? Schadenfreude?"

"Nice reference, Casey," said Jenna, "but remember, all things are God. That includes wickedness and the enjoyment thereof, especially, when you are God. God loves everything and everyone. God loves them because they are unique, each providing God with distinctively new and infinite ways to experience the physical universe. God takes pleasure in all of creation, don't you?"

I chuckled at my inability to adequately express my agreement with words, shrugged my shoulders, and simply said, "Yes!"

Jenna nodded approvingly and walked over to the whiteboard. She picked up the marker and underlined IT DON'T MATTER. "Everyone" she said, "ends up doing exactly what you are doing, no matter what. No matter how evil or how pious they may be in physical form – they all return to God. We are all one thing: God."

I blinked several times as I struggled to understand. "So, there is no Satan, no devil standing on peoples' shoulders whispering all manner of sinfulness in their ear?"

Jenna scoffed, "The devil is a contrivance that physical beings invented to explain the bad things they do. Many believe they do hear that voice, but it's their own limited minds. If they knew what you know now, they'd never even bother being bad, and that would be very bad for God. God needs people to be bad – and good. The whole point of existence is the battle. It is the conflict that provides the theater in which God may feel, and thereby know every possible way to be. It never gets old, it's always a little different, eternally unique and, for God, completely addicting and the only reason for which the universe was created."

Once again, the vast loneliness and emptiness I knew before the Big Bang overwhelmed me. What I'd experienced this morning as Jenna, as Fenny, and as Darlene was immeasurably superior. People talk about walking in another's shoes, but I'd been their souls! And yes, I wanted more, much more! Being was knowing, and I wanted to know everything! Omnicience was within my reach!

"I've only known three people!" I complained. "There are billions on Earth alone! And those are just the ones still alive! Oh! Oh! I know! Let me be the Nazi's and the Jews!"

"Easy, newbie, in fact, too easy. Most people have imagined both sides of that holocaust. There'll be plenty of time to revisit history once you graduate The OOO

Academy. We're going to a refugee camp in Bangladesh next. The Buddhists are trying to wipe out the Rohingya Muslims in Myanmar as we speak. If you got a kick out of one serial killer, you'll find modern-day ethnic cleansing nearly electrifying!"

Chapter 7: Bangladesh, Then Lunch

I woke to barking dogs and the unsteady braying of a hollowed sheep's horn calling all to Salat al-fajr, the first prayer before sunrise. "Awake, Jannatul!" called my mother, "Wash your self quickly, for God loves cleanliness!"

I sat up and rubbed the sleep from my eyes with my small, seven-year-old hands. Hunger rumbled in my tummy. I'd slept most of yesterday and all through the night. The dim light of approaching dawn barely illuminated our tiny hut made of bamboo and blue plastic tarpaulins. I'd slept under a thin sheet with a pillow fashioned from a bundle of rags. A small plastic bucket in the corner served as our toilet, and I hated it. It stunk but at least I didn't have to pee outside among the others. Mother was smiling as she watched me finish my business and praised me once again for my courage. She handed me a thick green cloth and motioned to another basin next to her pallet.

"That is clean water!" she said brightly. "Drink some before you wash!"

I cupped my hands and drank from them. This is good, I thought, not like the brackish, brown water that we'd been forced to drink during our long three-day walk to the camp. We'd arrived just yesterday morning, and my legs were still a bit rubbery from the weariness. I scrubbed my thickly calloused feet first, then washed up from there carefully as I'd been taught, finishing with my face and ears. I did it slowly, wincing often due to the myriad scratches, cuts, and bruises I'd sustained. My mind was numb, my meager energy burdened yet more by the lingering horror in my memory.

"Ah! Much better!" said Mother. "You are now as clean as your name! Come quickly now, before the sun peeks above the horizon!"

We left the shelter and joined the others on their way to the make-shift mosque. So much walking, what was another mile? As we rambled toward the clearing among many strangers, I couldn't help but recall the trauma of the past five days.

Our home in Myanmar had been simple and small, but it had electricity and indoor plumbing. We'd lived in a small Muslim community where everyone knew everyone else. A week ago, I'd known practically nothing of Buddhists. My father had always changed the subject if I asked. But when they came to our village it was as if demons had been loosed upon us. Last Monday evening was a night I'd never forget.

We'd finished our Salat al-'isha prayers and had been asleep for only a short time. I was awoken by my father calling to my mother, "Shahindra! They are coming! Quickly, take the girl and run to the forest!" I'd never heard fear in my father's voice before, and it frightened me terribly. My mother had whisked me from the bed, and we hurried from the house, her nearly dragging me by the arm. The alarm on her face caused tears of terror to spring from my eyes. We headed for the low wall at the back of our plot. "I'll boost you over!" whispered my mother frantically as we approached.

Just then, many angry voices and pounding footsteps rose from the other side of the wall, and my mother pulled me down to the ground, right up against the wall, and concealed us among the honeysuckle that grew there. She clasped her hand over my mouth, my eyes were wide with panic. While the men passed on the other side of the wall, we heard others shouting with such anger from inside our house. We watched frozen with fear as father ran out the back door with my two older brothers, Jakim and Sedera. Two men with automatic rifles popped out the door seconds later, and a hail of bullets brought down all three of them. My father and Sedera fell motionless. Jakim was screaming, his leg gushing blood. Four more men came around the house from the front wielding machetes. They fell upon Jakim and hacked at him in a beating frenzy, blood spraying in all directions.

Gunshots and screams rang out all around the village. Mother and I trembled violently, but silently in our hiding place. After slaughtering Jakim, the men quickly ran to Ghizsha's house next door and more screaming and shouting pierced the air before gunfire silenced them. A moment later, an explosion blew out the back wall. Debris rained upon the honeysuckle, someone's bloody hand landed just inches from our hiding place. I thought my heart would burst from my chest! What was happening? Who are these men? Why have they killed my father and brothers? Am I about to die?

When the men moved on to yet another house, my mother popped up quickly to peer over the wall. "Come now!" she whispered and threw me over the stones. I landed on my butt, but she was over and scooping me up before I could stand. "Run with me now to the trees, and ask God for protection!"

I didn't need any instruction. I ran faster than a cheetah being chased by a lion. The woods weren't far, and I noticed many others streaking toward the timbers, including a few of the village men, but mostly women with children and small babies, all running for their lives. Low limbs, bushes, and briars snagged at my arms, legs, and face as we tore through the dark forest. Women were weeping, children crying, and the men were shouting, "Run for the old temple! They won't look for us there!"

Just as I thought my heart would stop from sheer exhaustion we cleared the woods and saw the old Buddhist temple, an ancient ruin, long overgrown and crumbling. Still, it provided some shelter and a place to rest our pounding pulses. About twenty five of us huddled in a corner under what was left of the roof. The adults were trying to quiet the children. The stench of fear-provoked perspiration filled the air. Many had urinated in their clothing. Mothers held children tightly, their eyes wild with panic. Two of the men were praying in strangely stressed, but hushed tones. "Allah, protect us in our hour of need!"

I'd never questioned the mercy of God before, but watching those men chopping up my brother made me wonder if God really cared at all. What kind of God would allow his children to be butchered like dogs? What would cause such hatred in fellow human beings? At that moment, I understood, because I hated the men who had swung those machetes!

Mother and I selected a place to kneel among the gathered congregation at the make-shift mosque. As we chanted the ancient prayers, I did not feel comfort as I always had. The words rang hollow. Fresh tears streamed down my face. My father and brothers were gone, and I would never trust God again. I vowed to one day take revenge for their deaths.

* * *

Instantly, my Cern shifted from Jannatul to six Buddhist cleansers on that fateful Monday night. We were fit for slaughter, carrying AK-47's, machetes, hand grenades, and ropes. We crept up to the door of a Muslim home. Ahmed signaled to breach. Cedril, Malachi, and Faheed rammed the door with a huge bludgeon. It broke from its hinges and fell with a crash. Hassaan, Bojo and Ahmed rushed in, rifles spewing fire aimlessly. We were of one mind: kill the Muslim swine! Buddha will be glorified when we exterminate from our homeland these filthy pests. They were less than cockroaches and a danger to our own salvation.

Ahmed kicked open a bedroom door. The shrieking of three children was quickly silenced by a burst of gunfire. An adult male leaped from behind a sofa onto Bojo's back and stabbed at him with a steak knife. Hassaan whipped out his machete and, with a powerful pirouette, sliced off the man's head. Faheed dragged a woman by her hair from another bedroom. She was kicking and screaming and begging for her childrens' lives, which were already gone. Malachi took the woman's legs and together, he and Faheed carried her outside to a tree that stood close to the house. Ahmed flung a rope over a high branch. Cedril twisted several loops around the hysterical woman's neck and tied a triple knot. Ahmed and Hassaan pulled on the rope until the woman was dancing on her toes, unable to ease the pressure on her throat. Bojo took his revenge for the steak knife wound and rammed his machete into the Muslim's gut and twisted hard. Spasms ripped through her torso as he reached in, grabbed a handful of intestines, and yanked them from her. Ahmed and Hassaan pulled her higher off the ground and tied off the rope to a post near the front door of the house. We cheered and whooped as she swung there, writhing, gasping and bleeding out.

"Allah is a myth! There is no God! Does he save you now?" we taunted her mutilated and dying remains. "Hang there in your own tree and see if God saves you! We will kill you all, and eat your children for our dinner!" We laughed at her bulging eyes and swollen tongue. Crimson froth drooled from her mouth. We delighted in her death and mustered quickly toward another home.

* * *

The Cern ended abruptly. I was looking directly into Jenna's eyes which were dancing with delight. It took me a few seconds to speak. "OH! MY! GOD!!!" Jenna was nodding with exuberance, but stayed silent. "I had no idea!" I blurted. "Such fierce maternal love! Such unadulterated evil! Such deep and utter hatred! I thought that kind of thinking had been eradicated from the human race! But all six of those men – it was like they were a singular force completely devoid of compassion. I've never felt that way before. Fenny was a sadistic sonovabitch, but at least he was selective. But that, that was just…" I searched my vocabulary and could only come up with, "outstanding!" I laughed with intellectual understanding. My omniscience had grown by multiples with these latest seven Cernings.

"Being six people at once was one hell of a trip!" I proclaimed to Jenna.

"I knew you'd like it!" squealed Jenna.

"Jeez Jenna, you sound like that My Pillow guy again."

Confusion overtook her face and she asked, "I sound like that….what?"

"It's a commercial," I began and then realized "Oh. I'm sorry. You haven't watched much TV lately, have you?"

She looked at me askance and said "Casey, we don't need TV. When we Cern into people watching TV, we usually shift to someone more interesting, especially when the commercials come on."

"Good idea." I conceded.

"Who wants lunch?" called a voice from the door. Jenna and I jumped like we'd just touched a live electrical wire. We jerked our heads around and saw Abby skipping toward us carrying a large wicker hamper. She set it on the low table in front of our chairs. "I've brought a nice cucumber and tomato salad with raspberry dressing, summer sausages, some of mom's famous corn fritters, and blueberry Pop Tarts for dessert!"

This non sequitur event was so sudden that Jenna and I couldn't help but burst out laughing. Abby's puzzled face only made it funnier. "Did I interrupt something?" she asked.

"No, sweetie," assured Jenna, "we just weren't expecting you."

She looked at her mom cockeyed, then shrugged, and began dishing out the food. "So, Daddy, how do you like Cerning?"

I took a plate, reseated myself in my chair, and popped a sausage in my mouth. Talking as I chewed, I said "Well, it has been a learning experience, that's for sure." I jumped up and walked over to the cooler for a root beer. "Anyone want one?"

"You bet!" they both replied.

Quite a little family we were becoming! It made me feel warm and happy. I delivered a bottle to each and took a long swallow of my own. I dug back into my lunch, and after a moment said, "It's remarkable, you know, that people believe themselves to be so superior to others. I sort of knew that before, but having Cerned into those Buddhist beasts, it gave me a whole new understanding of narcissism. But the most disturbing thing I've learned so far is how destructive religion can be."

Abby was sitting cross-legged in front of our table facing us as she ate. "Yep," she agreed, "people have fought over the irrelevant since day one. It's probably the greatest secret of all. Then again, if they knew the truth, Cerning would be no fun at all. Nothing but rainbows and unicorns would defeat the whole purpose! Try those fritters, Daddy! They're delicious!"

Jenna chimed in "You'll find out first hand this afternoon, Casey, but you're catching on quickly! There are over forty three hundred religions currently being practiced just on Earth, and they all think theirs is the right one. It provides endless entertainment and emotional satisfaction."

I nodded in understanding. "I was only aware of the major religions before all this, and I knew they disagreed and often fought wars over their differences. I'm beginning to realize that God was really rather ingenious in providing an inkling of deity in everyone, but made them all think they had to work for the supposed rewards. I suppose, as a mortal being, any concept of God would seem supreme as well as separate. Little do they know that they are merely players on a stage before an audience of one."

"That would be us!" both Jenna and Abby agreed while motioning my inclusion in their statement.

"All for one, and one for all!" I chortled.

"E pluribus unum." said Jenna ironically. "That was so close! The notion that people are God's children was so close! People will always believe that they are separate from God and that only faith will keep them close, when in fact, they already are God and are merely vehicles by which God realizes and delights in his own creation. I've Cerned into enough psychologists to draw an analogy. Dissociative identity disorder is characterized by the presence of two or more distinct personality identities. Each may have a unique name, personal history, and characteristics. In some cases, one of those personalities is aware of all of the identities present. In that sense, God has trillions of personalities that are not aware of God, but God is aware of all of them."

"Good one, Mom!" Abby took on a crazed countenance. "I have a massive case of D.I.D. and am as crazy as a soup sandwich!"

"De unum multis!" I agreed. We all laughed merrily, enjoying our family lunch

When we finished eating, Abby cleared the table and vanished with her hamper after waving and saying, "See you back at the farm, Daddy!"

Jenna said with pride, "She's something else, isn't she?"

"A true blessing!" I agreed, "But I've been wondering. She was just an embryo when she got here, just about 24 hours before you did. How could she have gone through The OOO Academy without a developed brain?"

Jenna nodded knowingly. "Many ask that question as well as what about babies and toddlers who die. To a mortal, it seems quite impossible. But remember who we are and what we are capable of doing. For God, time is irrelevant. We don't age here as mortals, we pick a point of development. It can be any time during the mortal course of aging. Embryos, fetuses, newborns, infants, and toddlers all arrive at about five years of age. There's a whole separate school for them, and it's a bit different. They actually learn to Cern a little first and are able to accumulate five years of living experience almost immediately. Once they complete school, most choose to continue to age naturally until some point of adulthood. A few even revert back to infants to experience the entire growing process first hand. It's really quite remarkable, that school – we call it The COOO Academy."

I smiled at that. "The COOO Academy? For babies? That's adorable!"

Jenna giggled and smiled brightly. "Yeah, God has a wonderful sense of humor sometimes. The 'C' stands for Childhood Cerning, which we shorten to Cherning. They Chern first, then Melt, Cern, and..." she stopped herself, "well, let's not get ahead of ourselves. Anyway, I find it immensely rewarding to teach there often, and I think you will, too. There's quite a demand, you know. Just on Earth, and you'll find that most well-developed worlds are comparable, there are over forty million abortions every year – more than one every second. When the unfortunates who don't survive the first five years are added to the aborted, that number more than doubles. Fittingly, most of them end up choosing to teach new infant arrivals full time."

"Eighty million every year!?" I gasped.

"Yep, but they're special. Because they never really contribute much to God's sensory experience, having endured almost no trauma themselves, other than death, they become the most benevolent when interacting with mortals. Their personalities are irresistibly joyful – as you've seen!"

"That's amazing!" I said and thought for a moment. Jenna watched me expectantly as if she knew what I was about to ask. "They interact with mortals?"

Jenna laughed and sang "Tomorrow!"

I rolled my eyes, a bit disappointed. "Fine. So, what's next?"

"Over the next three hours, I'm cutting you loose! First, you'll Melt into everyone on Earth, then pick one person to Cern into. From that person, you will immediately Cern into the five closest people to the one you chose. Then, you'll Cern into the five closest to those five, and so on, until you've Cerned into everyone on Earth. You'll still be capped at that – we'll do the rest of the universe later as the last lesson today."

I was incredulous. "The whole planet?"

"Sure! You're going to be everyone. No sweat! Now, get comfortable in your chair, close your eyes, and when you're ready, cast your Melt."

I was a little nervous about the pending task, but I was also more than curious. Ever since I'd been those six Buddhist cleansers, I'd been hankering for another Cern. It had been like waiting for Christmas morning. I didn't know what I was going to get, but I was certain it would be thrilling. I sank back into the soft cushions of the generous chair, looked over at Jenna one last time. She nodded once and smiled sweetly, with love. It warmed my heart, and I returned both the smile and the nod. I closed my eyes and rested my head on the back of the chair.

Chapter 8: Becoming Everyone

I instantly Melted into everyone. I got that same feeling I had when I'd first done it with Abby. People were being added and subtracted at a phenomenal rate as people were born and died. It reminded me of that seemingly suspended and gushing water faucet I saw once at a Ripley's Believe It Or Not exhibit. But unlike that exhibit, the pool of lives did not remain constant. It slowly rose as births happened at a faster rate than deaths. Who does one choose to begin a worldwide Cern? Someone different from those I'd already been, someone different from me. Someone not too young and not too old. Someone with no apparent chance of dying soon.

I chose a trumpeter in the midst of a rehearsal of Rossini's William Tell Overture. I took a deep breath and willed the Cern. Mathematics, discipline, and an awareness of the strict control of embouchure flowed through me. I'd played this piece hundreds of times, but it never got old. The opening andante was finally coming to a conclusion, and I set my eyes on the conductor awaiting his cue to begin the exciting allegro that most people associate with The Lone Ranger theme. As it began, my Cern expanded into the entire trumpet section, four guys and a gal. We stood and began the heralding bugle call: Ta Ta Tah! Ta Ta Tah! I could feel the sense of ensemble each player felt, and the pride they took in being collectively concise, perfectly on pitch, and exciting the prospective audience.

Within three measures, I'd Cerned into the entire orchestra, the conductor, and two janitors that had stopped their sweeping backstage to listen to their favorite part. One of the janitors, nearing retirement, was envisioning Clayton Moore as the Lone Ranger, galloping on his trusty steed exclaiming "Hi-O Silver". He'd loved that TV show he watched as a toddler.

But my Cern continued to expand to the administrative and sales people working at Symphony Hall. One woman was tediously typing at a computer processing accounts receivable while being distracted over the worry of her son having a tonsillectomy tomorrow. A young man hooted as he closed the sale of 50 season tickets. "That's my quota!" he yelled to his co-workers.

I held on to all those people as my Cern quickly snowballed to the people on the sidewalks and parking lots surrounding the building, then to the drivers and passengers in cars, trucks, and buses on Huntington and Massachusetts Avenue. Before the orchestra had gotten to the 'titty rump titty rump titty rump rump rump' part, I'd Cerned into everyone in Boston. I became executives, housewives, construction workers, clergy, meth addicts, wife beaters, nurses, jockeys, librarians, thieves, politicians, policemen, life guards, football players, paramedics, plumbers, college students, paraplegics, mechanics, and more children than you could shake a Pop Tart at. I absorbed their souls and knew their secrets. I felt a grand expanse of emotion ranging from stalwart loyalty to bitter hatred. I knew their tedium, their striving, their disappointment, their success, their charity of heart, their sense of community, and their penchant for power. I was minds of every description, from the ignorant to the genius, from the autistic to the curious, from the conniving to the contrite, and everything in between. It was a glorious feeling to be them all, all at once! It felt right, and good, and so, so satisfying!

My Cern quickly expanded to all of Massachusetts and into New York, Connecticut, New Hampshire, Rhode Island, and Vermont. I became lumber jacks, lobstermen, railroad engineers, hermits, trailer trash, sailors, and marines. I was doctors, scholars, psychics, pilots, soccer goalies, lonely old men, missionaries, strippers, firemen, peeping toms, anarchists, judges, and juries. Every personality, history, and mind was unique!

I willed my Cern ever further, and by the time the orchestra's percussion section was pounding out the final crashing measures of the Overture, I'd Cerned into all of North America and well into the Southern Hemisphere. I soon knew the hearts and minds of dictators, peasants, slum lords, drug traffickers, jungle guides, gold miners, assassins, ditch diggers, spies, presidents, bailiffs, killers, and people addicted to every substance, activity, and idea imaginable as well as several things I'd never imagined.

The orchestra was now pounding on tonic like a blacksmith high on ecstasy as my Cern jumped the Bering Straits and flooded into Asia like a tsunami. I Cerned into souls in China, the Koreas, Japan, India, Pakistan, through Turkey, and into Europe. I washed over Africa, and by the time the orchestra finally fell quiet, I'd hopped into Australia, Hawaii, Greenland, and Iceland. In less than twenty minutes, I had every soul on Earth under surveillance, and I felt magnanimous! I was God, and I was with everyone!

With such a comprehensive view of humanity came a multitude of surprising revelations. It became clear that the older people were, the more they were burdened with negative thoughts, emotions, and inclinations. Pride was the most prolific sensation. People used reward systems to instill it in children at very early ages. There was no limit to the things, thoughts, responses, and events that evoked that feeling in people. It could be as innocuous as having brushed one's hair to satisfaction. Achieving long sought goals produced powerful feelings of pride, superiority, narcissism, and megalomania.

Greed showed up a lot, too, from hungry babies to shopaholics, to business owners, mayors, drug kingpins, charitable organizations, insurance companies, and entire countries who fought over natural resources. People conjured simple to complex webs of lies and deceit in an attempt to gain more than their competitors and took great pride in having done so. They rewarded themselves and each other in their accomplishments and took great pride in their victories.

In their pursuit of pride driven by greed, individuals would often resort to anger, wrath, and murder to achieve their ends. Husbands beat their wives when sex was withheld or the pot roast wasn't to their liking. As hit men, I murdered people for other people to feed my own greed for money, position, pride, reputation, and power. As spoiled children, I threw tantrums, broke things, and assaulted weaker kids to acquire my desires. Nearly one third of the planet engaged in daily vitriol toward one another on social media, television, radio, and in print. Thousands of riots, demonstrations, and protests raged continuously all around the globe fueling even greater numbers to share the rage and take pride in whatever cause they deemed worthy.

Timid individuals would envy those who took action, who dared to attempt or succeed in realizing their most fervent wishes. Most people were fanatics about multiple things, famous people, ideologies, and even colors, music, rocks, and toys. Jealousy was rampant in all souls. Even clergy pined for sex and assailed the small, the weak, and the vulnerable in surreptitious circumstances to satisfy that envy. As thieves, I would concoct elaborate plans to steal the things that other people had and many times would kill to avoid capture.

The human race's innate desire to survive was fueled by copious thoughts of and desires for sex. Lust drove half the decisions made by young adults. Men payed for it, and women's greed charged plenty for the opportunity. Sensual pleasure was sought more often than food and drink by some people. I performed in all manners of lascivious activity. Both verbal and body language was fraught with sexual innuendo. I paid large sums of money to clothing, cosmetic, and drug companies to make myself more attractive. I mutilated my body with silicone implants, penile enhancements, piercings, and tattoos. I endured slavery, as both men and women were kept for the sole purpose of providing sexual pleasure and satisfying the lust of their owners or their owner's patrons. Some people took it so far as to assign sexual value to inanimate objects such as cars, shoes, earrings, and wigs.

The majority of the planet was overweight and many of those were morbidly so. In most countries food was more than abundant. Half of the planet was eating something every second. I was convinced that big was beautiful and mounted campaigns to shame those who shamed gluttony. I peddled a huge variety of weight loss programs to those gluttons and gleefully took their money as they purchased exercise machines, expensive running shoes, and weeks at fat farms. Advertisements, commercials, and road signs appealing to taste buds were ubiquitous. Diabetes and heart disease weakened many. Cholesterol clogged arteries enriched both pharmaceutical companies, surgeons, and ultimately funeral homes and cemeteries. One quarter of the people I Cerned into drank as much alcohol as they did water. Far too many of me were inebriated at any given time.

And so many people were simply lazy and slothful. Apathy and lethargy afflicted many, and quite a few did little more than stare at LED screens throughout my afternoon Cern. Some people lay and listened to music for hours. Some would merely sit and read. People drove half a mile instead of walking. They took escalators and elevators instead of the stairs. They put their dogs on long leads tied to their homes instead of properly walking them. Some men would use a bottle to pee in so they didn't have to get up and go to the bathroom. Comfort and idleness ravaged many minds, and inactivism ruled their day.

I was astonished at the pervasive wickedness of nearly half the human souls I Cerned. They schemed and lied, stole and killed, gorged, and did nothing useful. Hatred glowed bright red in much of humanity, and a good deal of it was actually self-loathing. Stress and depression was rampant. I went to great lengths and huge expense to assuage my misery. I consumed all sorts of pills, paid psychiatrists, talked to therapists, and poisoned my body and mind in an attempt to soothe my earthly loneliness and suffering. It all reminded me of my own suffering, before the Big Bang.

But to my surprise, I also learned that tons of people were generally and genuinely humble, meek, and modest. Cheerfulness, love, and a deep caring for others motivated the decisions of many people. They loved themselves and others deeply. They were loyal and forgiving. A great number of people were driven by a strong sense of vicarity, the closest a mortal can get to Cerning, marked by strong empathy and sympathy. I put myself in the shoes of others and was energetic in my motivation to help, serve, comfort, and alleviate their problems. I was focused on their needs, instead of mine.

Much of the planet was noble, compassionate, and peaceful. There were people everywhere who were honest, respectful, courageous, forgiving, and kind. They did the right thing and didn't bend to impulses, urges or desires, but acted according to decent values and principles. Many had practical wisdom, were streetwise and savvy, and demonstrated authenticity and moral authority.

I enjoyed immensely being firefighters, law enforcement of all kinds, religious leaders, physicians, surgeons, nurses, physical therapists, laborers of all kinds, customer service representatives, sales people, and honest merchants. It was thrilling to rescue children from burning buildings, exciting to apprehend heinous criminals, rewarding to guide people to more inner peace, gratifying to cure deadly diseases, and satisfying to complete the construction of a beautiful home. I rid buildings of bugs, eradicated computer viruses, and invented new ways to make life easier for millions. I organized people to feed the hungry, shelter the homeless, and provide companionship for the elderly.

It was utterly stunning when my Cern swept through Atlanta and engulfed Alicia, Brenda, my mother, the colleagues I worked with and all the people I'd ever interacted with throughout the city. It had only been two days since my murder. Given the notoriety of the Ramos case, the media were camped out in front of our house, hoping to interview Alicia. My boss, Frank, had arranged significant security for her and Brenda. The men who'd attacked us had been apprehended and, of course, I Cerned into them as well. They were a cousin of the man Ramos had killed and two henchmen he'd engaged to assist in the assassination. Incredibly, they were as satisfied with their deed, despite their probable and eventual execution, as I was satisfied by experiencing their satisfaction!

Alicia was morose with grief, but stoically plodding through my final arrangements with Jordon Calloway, our family attorney, on the phone. Poor Brenda was curled up under her covers on her bed, sad and confused. My mother was in our kitchen trying to prepare some dinner for everyone, her eyes moist and hollow, her movements lacking enthusiasm. All their hearts were broken, their attitudes angry, but subdued. I soaked it all in, and even though I felt every nuance of their anguish, that misery made my Divine Soul glad inasmuch as it allowed me to feel what the void before the Big Bang could never have delivered.

As my Cern continued into the third hour, it became clear to me that every interaction between people, no matter how good or how bad was counterbalanced by the opposite; there was a right for every wrong and a wrong for every right. Helping one person necessarily required ignoring another. The purchase of life-saving medication enriched greedy drug companies. I stole cars and sold their parts, but used the money to pay for my child's education. I murdered pedophiles and spared children that future trauma. I beautified a home with new vinyl siding, but threw the homeowner into bankruptcy. I gave money to beggars who used it to purchase drugs on which they overdosed. No matter which starving nation I shipped food to, the people in the nations I did not choose perished from hunger. I poisoned my husband, thus preventing him from driving drunk and T-boning a bus full of elementary students with his Humvee. No good deed went unpunished, and every cloud had a silver lining. There was a constant battle within people and in every interaction between good and evil. Ultimately, it was a wash; morality and immorality were at loggerheads – an eternal tug of war – neither side gaining a permanent advantage. No matter what anyone did, in the end, it simply didn't matter to the continuum of humanity.

But as God, to experience it all, from every point of view was utterly exhilarating! I felt myself flowing into every conception and exiting every death. I delighted in every person, no matter what they did, good or bad. To be, to feel, to love, to hate, to suffer, to laugh, to cry, to endure every success and every failure was all-consuming, awe-inspiring, and totally addicting. I was in a continual state of excitement and expectation, hanging on the edge of anticipation during every second of every life. And it was goddam good!! I never wanted this ride to end!

* * *

But it did end, more abruptly than it had started. Jenna stood before me, her loving gaze engaging mine. I was still in my chair there in the Omniscient classroom. I was no longer lounging; I was sitting with a straight spine, on the edge of my seat, feet flat on the floor, eyes wide with wonderment. My hands gripped the arms of my chair firmly, and I was breathing fast and hard. My heartbeat was rapid and strong.

"Relax, Casey," said Jenna soothingly, "Relax."

I seemed to be frozen in my posture, but my breathing and heartbeat were slowing. When I was finally able to focus on Jenna, all I could whisper was, "Shit fire and save matches!"

Jenna burst out laughing, and I looked at her like she'd just grown a third arm. "What's so funny?" I asked, a giggle beginning in my belly.

"People say a lot of things when they drop out of their first global Cern, but I've never heard that one before! Shit fire and save matches! That's a good one!" she sputtered through her continuing glee. "You ought to see your face right now!" By then, I was laughing uncontrollably myself, happy with Jenna, delighted with humanity, and joyful to be God.

Chapter 9: Dinner And A Gallop

As we walked back to the farm for dinner, I chattered incessantly, trying to tell Jenna all about what I had experienced that afternoon. She remained mostly silent, but attentive and happily engrossed in my exuberance. By the time we walked into the kitchen I was going on and on about how many languages I could now speak.

Abby was setting the last of the food on the table as we entered. She said, "Guten Abend Papa! Wie war dein globales Cern?"

"Es war gut, Tochter! Zehr gut!! Ausgezeichnet!" I exclaimed.

"I knew you'd like it!" she tittered. "I hope you're hungry! I made chicken and dumplings, a green bean casserole, cornbread muffins, and a scrumptious apple crisp for dessert!"

The kitchen was thick with tantalizing aromas and my mouth was watering. I found that I had an enormous appetite; apparently, global Cerning was hard work! "It smells delicious! Let's eat!"

We all sat down at the table, but before I could say "Pass the beans" Jenna and Abby chanted, "Being God is great, being God is good! Cerning's hard work and requires a lot of food!" I grinned in amazement.

"Say it with us, Daddy!" encouraged Abby.

I joined right in, "Being God is great, being God is good! Cerning's hard work and requires a lot of food!" Abby laughed with delight. Jenna and I joined in the merriment.

The conversation was easy and good-humored throughout the meal. We each talked about our first global Cerns and how amazing they had been. Having acquired the collective knowledge of the entire population of Earth was something that you never ran out of things to talk about. Abby would tell stories about animals and could lecture at any zoo exhibit. Jenna would go on and on about cooking, with particular interest in Asian recipes. What seemed to impress me the most about what I'd learned was the way in which different cultures, and the communities within those cultures, interpreted the laws by which they lived. As Abby served dessert, I began a small dissertation comparing the draconian totalitarianism of North Korea to the extremely libertarian Finnish people.

The sun was nearing the horizon by the time Jenna began clearing away the dishes and leftovers from the table. "Now that you're an excellent equestrian, what do you say we take a twilight ride?"

"You have horses?" I asked with excitement.

She grinned, "We sure do! We'll take Ole Billy and Maple out for a twilight run!" She shot Abby a glance.

"Yeah!" said Abby, "You kids go have fun. I'll do the dishes!" She smiled innocently. I shook my head with wonder. My two girls shared some sort of unspoken language I had yet to learn!

Ole Billy turned out to be a jet black stallion with a cream-colored mane and front stockings. Jenna explained he was only twelve years old, despite his name. She saddled up Maple, a brown sugar filly with gentle eyes. We mounted up and walked them out of the barn down a gravel path through a gate in the bullwire fencing that enclosed the pasture. Once we cleared the gate, Jenna kicked Maple in the ribs and started off at a trot. "C'mon Casey!" she hollered.

I whooped, "Hyah!!" and Ole Billy responded immediately. It took a few seconds to catch up to Maple and Jenna, but before we could pull ahead, she urged Maple into a canter. Ole Billy required no instruction and nearly mirrored the timing of Maple's gait. We whooped with glee as we followed the riding trail over rolling hills that emptied into a broad flat plain. I spotted a rock formation about a mile ahead, and spurring Ole Billy into a gallop, shouted, "Last one there's a cross-eyed Panda!!"

"We'll see about that!" screamed Jenna over the pounding hooves.

The lead changed several times before the rock formation began to loom large. I grimaced, quads begging for rest from squeezing the saddle, but Ole Billy seemed to want to win, hooves pounding the ground in an incessant staccato. Jenna surged up behind us, Maple's nose even with my knees. Both horses were panting hard, nostrils flaring with each breath. The trail opened into a dusty birth at the base of the rocks. Maple had pulled up nose to nose with Ole Billy. When we hit the dust, Ole Billy turned left and slowed down fast. Maple turned right and slowed to a trot as well. Jenna steered him in a circle to come back around to me and Ole Billy. As she drew nigh, she looked over at me with crossed eyes and said with a goofy face, "Who's a panda, huh?!"

I snorted almost as loudly as Ole Billy, made a cartoonish face myself and sang, "I'm a cross-eyed Panda!" in a moronic voice. Our laughter echoed off the rocks, but not for long. Jenna and I were as winded as the animals.

Still atop the horses, at a walk, Jenna led us around the rock formation and up a slight rise. A stream ran down from somewhere above the rocks and cut through the rise. Small trees grew along its bank, and that's where we finally dismounted and tethered the horses where they could drink from the stream.

It was dusk, the sun had set and stars were becoming bright in the night sky. A crescent moon was a few degrees above the horizon. Jenna took my hand and said, "Come with me. I want to show you something." She wore a tempting smile.

When we breached the crest of the rise and could see what was beyond, my jaw dropped, my eyes got as big as communion wafers. A long, satisfied "Ohhhh!" escaped me as I panned the view.

We were standing at the edge of an enormous crater that must have been made millions of years ago. It stretched beyond visibility to both sides and sloped gently down from where we stood to an unfathomable depth. The stream spilled over the lip and fell into the void. A wispy mist rose from the darkness below. The Milky Way sparkled before us more brightly, more robustly, and more intensely, than I'd thought possible. It was as if we were standing on the edge of the world, millions of stars even appeared lower than we. Jenna found a spot near the waterfall that was covered with thick spongy moss and said softly, "Have a seat."

Chapter 10: Among The Stars

I couldn't take my eyes off the astronomical view. Slowly, I dropped to a cross-legged sitting position. She sat behind me, her legs on either side, her arms around my chest, her chin nestled on my shoulder. She talked softly in my ear. "You are God. This is your universe. Become it, be it, know it now."

* * *

I instantly Melted into every bit of physical matter in existence, then, Praise Me, I Cerned into every living soul within it!! Jenna held me firmly as I became everyone everywhere.

The people I became were as similar to Earthlings as one color is to its nearest gradient, but like the light spectrum, were of infinite variety and hue. Some worlds were sparsely populated with relatively primitive beings, while others were much more crowded than Earth and contained societies more advanced.

There was something very different about this Cern, though. It wasn't just myself Cerning the masses. Jenna was there, too, but, moreover, there were millions of other Divine Personalities riding the lives of each and every individual. I understood that no one was ever alone, no matter how isolated they assumed they were. God was with them at all times, as multiple Divine Beings initiated and dissolved their personal Cerns.

People everywhere had at least some notion of God, but, of course, no one knew the truth. It was breathtaking to realize that conflict and love were at the heart of every mortal soul, but in such constantly novel combinations that each individual brought new admiration and riveting pleasure to me. The stories of their lives were not unfamiliar, yet each was unique. My gratification amplified beyond measure.

I knew everything there was to know, but with each passing second, my people discovered, invented, and realized billions of new things about themselves, each other, the world on which they lived, and about the laws of physics that provided the infrastructure for it all. Above all else, I understood why I designed the universe in such a way that no one would ever travel near the speed of light, much less exceed that. They must never know of each other, of how similar they were, of how conflict was crucial to my everlasting indulgence. They must never understand that they always returned to from whence they came. They must never know that I did this all for me and not for them, that in fact, they were merely brief, relatively ignorant, embodied reiterations of me, consisting solely of me, created solely for my own amusement and delectation. How could I not love them all? They were me, and I was them.

* * *

When the Cern evaporated, the moon was near its zenith and the constellations had shifted westward. Jenna still hugged me from behind, rocking us both slightly back and forward. In unison, we whispered, "We love us all."

We basked in the afterglow of our Cern for several long minutes. The day had been long and more than a little exhausting. It was warm and comfortable in Jenna's arms, and I wanted little more than to simply sleep, but a question was nagging at me. There was still one mystery I realized had not been solved. "Jenna," I queried, "we just Cerned the entire universe, but nowhere did I see us, Abby, Bob or this place. I didn't find the farm, the schools, any dinosaurs anywhere, the horses, the stream or anything I've seen since arriving. This place is not on Earth or any other world. Where are we?"

Her answer was a cryptic question. "Where do you go in your dreams?"

I considered for a long moment before saying "Nowhere. Anywhere. Familiar places, strange places. It's all in my head, yet as real as anything actually experienced."

Jenna remained silent as I continued to ponder. "Many psychologists believe the mind cannot distinguish between a real and an imagined event. They say that if you could imagine playing the piano vividly enough, without ever having practiced, one could conceivably play Clair De Lune." I shrugged a bit and asked "Is this all a dream? What I imagined heaven would be? But that can't be entirely right. I would never have imagined Abby, and I'd been convinced you'd ran off to South America or had been abducted, murdered, and disposed of in parts unknown. I never considered your suicide, so how could I have imagined that incredible Cern into you?"

Jenna continued rocking me ever so gently, but said nothing. I continued with my analysis. "I am God. If I can conjure up an entire universe, I can also invoke an afterlife for everyone that is simultaneously both real and imagined! It would include familiar places, faces, and activities in an environment worthy of a life after death, just as one might imagine it to be. But it would also be full of wonderment and resolution of all problems and mysteries." I chuckled softly, "The chicken and dumplings Abby made were as real as food gets! And there is no way I could ever imagined knowing how to find oil, engineer a satellite or land a fighter jet on an aircraft carrier, but I can do those things and so much more now!"

Jenna continued to rock, as steady as a ticking clock, but remained mute. I came to my own conclusion, "This place is where we are, as we wish it to be. It's a place that doesn't exist in the physical universe, yet mimics it in every respect. It is nowhere that mortals could ever go, but where Divine Beings can be comfortable and happy while enjoying all the physical universe has to offer. It is God's place, our place, my space."

Jenna finally spoke while still rocking us rhythmically. "It's like cyberspace. You know it exists, but GPS fails to find a route."

That was worthy of at least a giggle, but my weariness was pulling sweet sleep across my conscience, and all I could manage was an agreeable "Mmmm" as I drifted off to sleep.

Chapter 11: Omnipotence

The same rooster was crowing the next morning. I opened my eyes to find myself back in the same cozy bedroom I'd slept in the night before. I wondered briefly if I'd find Jenna lying next to me, but I was alone. I sat up on the edge of the bed and noticed a fresh pitcher of root beer, still foamy with carbonation, a new bucket of ice and two blueberry Pop Tarts on a plate setting on the nightstand. This time there was a folded note next to the plate with 'Daddy' written on it. I picked it up and opened the fold.

Good morning, Daddy! Here are some Pop Tarts and root beer for you. Today is the last day of school, and I will be so proud of you at your graduation this evening! Love you so much! ~ Abby

That child! A broad smile overtook my face. Love and warmth flooded through me. I felt amazingly refreshed and energy was surging through my body. The past two days had been miraculous, and I could hardly wait to see what Omnipotence School would bring. Melting and Cerning were powerful skills, but apparently there was an overreaching ability yet to be learned. As I munched on the Pop Tarts, their sweet aroma was mingled with something much more musky. It took me a moment to realize I smelled like a horse! Of course! I laughed out loud at myself, and with a pastry in hand, walked to the bathroom and turned on the shower. When the water got steamy, I stepped in and let the soft spray wash over me. I found a marvelous bottle of body wash that reminded me of sunshine and summer breezes. I scrubbed myself thoroughly, shampooed my hair, and took an extra minute to allow the massage setting to pound my shoulders and back. By the time I toweled dry and donned a fresh set of clothing, I felt like I was ready for anything. I combed my hair and winked at myself in the mirror, walked to the bedroom door, and turned the knob.

The door opened to a room quite unlike any classroom I'd ever seen. There was no blackboard or whiteboard, no lectern, no padded chairs or sofa, and no buffet. That was disappointing; I was as hungry as a polar bear adrift on an ice floe! The Pop Tarts had only whetted my appetite. The room didn't even have walls or a floor or a ceiling. It was a perfect sphere, as though I'd stepped inside a giant, white beach ball. At the core of the sphere above me floated, slightly and slowly bobbing, a throne. It faced away from me. As it ever so leisurely began to rotate toward me, to my astonishment, I began to levitate, on a direct path to the chair. My heart was pounding with expectation and excitement. Who would be sitting in the chair? Bob? Some stranger? The Pope? Jesus Christ? The God of all Gods?

The seat came into view as my body drew nigh to it. It was empty! My eyes popped with surprise, but my body was turning, and a few seconds later I was seated on the throne. Without anything by which to judge perspective, I couldn't tell if the chair was still rotating or not. I could no longer discern the limits of the sphere. The white boundaries of the orb surrounded me at some indecipherable distance. It was eerily quiet. Nothing was happening. I was utterly intrigued, but held complete faith in the ability of the afterlife to dazzle me. I searched the emptiness surrounding me with eager anticipation.

I jumped when a strong, masculine, curious voice sounded, "God Almighty, what is Thy will?"

"Jeezy weezy!" I exclaimed. I whipped my head all around but found no source of the voice. I gathered myself with a crooked smile and said, "Ok, fine. What is my will? How about...three eggs scrambled with cheese, a short stack of blueberry pancakes, maple syrup, a double order of bacon, and a large orange juice." As I spoke each item, they appeared on a table laid across the arms of my throne.

"Oh! Now, that is way cool!" I exclaimed, with one last look around, seeing no one. I picked up golden cutlery and dug into my meal. I began eating with gusto, shoveling bite after bite into my mouth. A drop of syrup dripped onto my shirt. "A napkin would be nice." I thought. A napkin appeared in my left hand. "Huh!" I said out loud, tucked the large, silver cloth under my chin, and continued my breakfast.

The bacon was perfectly crisp, just the way I like it, and the orange juice – fresh and pulpy! I finished the meal in short order and leaned back in my throne, satiated and feeling even better. I was ready to get on with it and wished there was somewhere to set the little table tray and empty plates. They vanished.

I waited a moment or two, but nothing else happened. Speculation seemed unproductive, so I commanded directly, "I want the instructor."

A large translucent face appeared before me. Beams of light radiated around it, obscuring any torso or limbs it might have had. It appeared to be a mature, but not old man, with flowing brown hair and kind eyes. His face was clean shaven, but otherwise expressionless. I had Cerned into everyone in the universe, but this face was unfamiliar. He was obviously a Divine Being. "Who are you?" I asked.

In an even and objective voice that oozed with charm he said, "I am that I am."

"Aw, c'mon, man!" I complained, "That's just plain cheesy!"

"So were your eggs." he retorted without derision.

I squinted my eyes and cocked my head to the left. He'd simply stated a fact. He didn't react to my expression which changed to a raised left eyebrow – Spock-like. He didn't react to that, either.

"That's it? That's all you have to say: 'So were your eggs'? I wish you had a bit more personality, Bud!"

His expression instantly became more animated and, well, normal. "Congrats, Casey! You've successfully completed Lesson One of Omnipotence School!"

That took me aback! "I did?" I asked incredulously.

"Sure! Here, you may prod at will. You picked that up right off the bat with your breakfast, and now, by giving me personality." He was smiling.

"Prod? You mean like a cattle prod? What are you talking about?" I asked, checking the area for cows.

"Close! But no cigar, my friend. Prodding is defined as the gentle manipulation of inanimate objects. Here, you can even do it with animate objects, but not with conscience-bearing beings." He nodded in agreement with himself.

"Not with conscience-bearing beings? Why not? If I'm omnipotent, I should be able to do anything I want!"

"Oh, you can, but you don't want to."

"How do you know what I want?" I demanded.

"Because I am you, and you are me, and since you are me, and I know what I don't want, so do you."

I looked at him with utter bafflement and shook my head vigorously, cheeks flapping. "What!??"

He chortled with merriment. "Don't worry about that right now. I love to confuse newbies. It's a character flaw."

I looked at him askance and said, "I thought God was perfect."

"You are. Even your flaws are perfect."

I rolled my eyes. This was going nowhere fast. "Don't you have a lecture or something to deliver?" I asked.

He sighed with disappointment. "Very well. Sit back and listen up."

"That's more like it." I commended, settling back in my throne.

"As you know, omnipotent means all-powerful. Only God is omnipotent. You have the ability to do whatever you want. You can create and destroy universes or any part thereof. You can create life. You can kill life. You can even make a rock so big that you yourself cannot lift it, but that would be pointless, as you discovered in the first universe you created."

"The first universe? How many…"

"Shhhh!!!! Don't interrupt! But yes, there were thousands of universes before you finally got everything just right. Perfection takes time! While experimenting with those earlier universes you came to understand what worked and what didn't. You fine-tuned the laws of physics until you created a process by which evolution would finally produce the conscience-bearing mortal beings with endless emotions that you enjoy being so much. Trust me, you don't want to mess that up!"

I was already hankering for at least a galactic Cern. "Boy, you got that right!" I agreed.

"Don't interrupt!" He arched his eyebrows with warning. I clamped my mouth shut. He continued, "You learned to allow people free will, for that is what produces the most intense emotions and maximum enjoyment for you. You learned not to implant thoughts, but to be surprised by what they think, say, and do. As the infinite variety of mortals pass into Divine Beings, they retain their personalities, and that is what guides any prodding they may do. As I mentioned, you may amuse yourself by gently manipulating inanimate objects in the mortal world. For instance, you could create a pothole in a road that creates an accident and all the emotions that follow from that event. Conversely, you could create an oasis to save someone lost in the dessert.

"While on Earth you undoubtedly prayed a lot, or at least were aware of billions of people who did. While you were Cerning yesterday, you heard those prayers, not just from Earthlings, but from all people everywhere. They have many specific ideas about what you may or may not allow, do or change. As you discovered, the intensity of emotion that accompanies those prayers are immensely pleasurable. Therefore, you allow them to believe that whatever happens is your will – thy will be done – and all that jazz. But if you imposed your will on just one person, it would snowball into a consummate debacle as you learned in the universe before this one. Go ahead, think back now, and review your chagrin."

I blinked several times and traveled eons back into the past, long before our Big Bang, to a universe fraught with destruction – a result of my misguided meddling in mortal affairs. I cringed at that memory that quickly rolled back in time through countless other universal failures.

He went on. "The penultimate universe ended with boring universal hatred. You destroyed every last mortal and Divine Being it produced and languished in a deep, lonely depression for the longest time. You'd thought you'd gotten it right, but you wouldn't entertain the notion of mortal free will. When it finally dawned on you what was necessary, you burst into the current, and finally perfect, universe. You vowed to yourself to never, ever implant a thought or notion into any mortal, conscience-bearing being.

"But you can influence inanimate objects, within the realm of physical laws, to give people the opportunity to choose their response, and thus their emotions. People get in a rut sometimes and become boring to be. It's amazing what a simple flat tire can produce! Or a jammed handgun. Or an infestation of cockroaches.

"As you discovered during your Cern yesterday, there are trillions of Divine Beings Cerning individuals at any given time. Each of them have the same omnipotence as you, but all abide by the vow of free will you will take. Furthermore, they all understand that anything they might do that would end the universe would also end them, as it did in the last one. So, no messing with the laws of physics!

There are plenty of naturally dying stars and civilizations to satisfy even the most sadistic of Divine Beings. There's no need to unnaturally instigate super-volcanoes, massive asteroid impacts or life-destroying solar flares. Be patient – they'll happen all by themselves, and if you're into that level of mortal despair and horror, it's quite the rush!

"Many Divine Beings spend eons satisfied with simple Melting and Cerning. Prodding is possible, and everyone experiments from time to time, but in general, it simply isn't necessary. Mortals have a knack for causing all sorts of things, both good and bad, devastating and miraculous, without any help from us.

Now then," he went on, "here, among ourselves, you can do as you wish without regard to the laws of physics, because as you figured out last night in Jenna's arms, we are not physical beings, and this is not a physical location. You can make things appear, vanish or change location at will. It doesn't matter as everything is as we wish. If one of us goes too far, we each have the ability to instantly reverse, correct or terminate the offensive attempt. But, by and large, we use our power to make each other more comfortable here, make things more convenient, like when breakfast appeared, and the mess of it vanished, or you floating in this silly throne, or me just being a head."

The man smiled with satisfaction and stopped talking. The lecture had been mesmerizing and completely captivating. As he'd explained the finer points of omnipotence, I'd found myself Cerning through history and verifying everything he said. Yesterday, I'd lost count of the times I would have liked to help or hinder people in their choices and endeavors, and had found myself looking forward to learning how to do just that. Despite what I'd just learned and verified, the notion of manipulating lives was still an intoxicating fantasy. So many times, I'd wished I could grant the prayers of the sad, wounded or oppressed. I still wanted to try something!

It was as if he could read my mind (of course he could, he was me!) and he said, "Of course you do, and so you shall, for it is the second lesson today: Prod a mortal to realize that it simply doesn't matter."

I felt like I'd just been given permission to rob a bank with impunity. "Really?" I asked excitedly, "I can do something now?"

"Sure, knock yourself out."

His flippant attitude gave me pause, but the mischievous urge within me was too strong to resist. Still, I didn't want to upset the apple cart too much. I searched the memory of my global Cern and settled on a widow, named Mabel Rosenfeld in Cleveland, Ohio. The entire region had been suffering an unusual and long draught. The roses she'd planted in the garden bed in front of her house had wilted. Her only income was social security, and she feared that watering them would render her water bill too high to pay. She had prayed for rain. A simple, three-hour steady drizzle ought to bring out the bloom in both her roses and her smile. So, I made it rain!

Mabel was overjoyed when she saw the first drops splattering on her sidewalk. She took up a position in a lawn chair she kept on her front porch to savor the welcome rain. She praised me as it fell, and that really felt good! Having Cerned into her, the roses, her poodle Oodles, and every other living thing on her property, I enjoyed the rejuvenation of all the plants in addition to her own delight which her dog innately shared. The rain also rejuvenated the mosquitos residing on her property. Several of them carried the virus that causes heartworms in canines. Two of them deposited the virus in poor little Oodles. I Melted deep within the dog's anatomy and biochemistry, and immediately realized the dog would ultimately succumb to the disease, leaving poor Mabel completely alone.

Undoubtedly, some of the more callous Divine Beings would prefer the impending misery the dog's death would cause Mabel, but for me, it was an unwelcomed consequence of my granting her prayers. Assuredly, I too derived as much pleasure from negative emotions as I did positive, but my intent had been foiled.

"See what I mean?" said the head.

Yeah," I admitted, "but can't I go back and do something to get rid of the mosquitos before I make it rain?"

"Nope. No do-overs. You can't change history, well, you can, but you learned not to do that a hundred universes ago. Check it out."

I Cerned back through history once again and saw the mayhem that changing history could cause. "Got it." I sighed.

"If you're ever in doubt about the wisdom of prodding, always look to the past for examples of how it's turned out before. Most Divine Beings soon realize that it doesn't matter. It has no effect on the cumulative balance of emotions you'll enjoy by simply Cerning. There will always be a few that mess around prodding this and that, and you'll enjoy the consequences of their mischief, but most don't bother at all."

I contemplated that for a moment and then asked, "So...why not prohibit prodding altogether, like changing history, influencing free will, or changing the laws of physics?"

"Excellent question! Jenna said you were quick on the draw!" His eyes twinkled as he admired his student. "Because Casey, for us it is irrelevant and harmless. It changes nothing in the grand scheme of things, and whatever the results may be, we all enjoy the ensuing reactions of every mortal affected. Consider it a divinely sinful indulgence. It's kind of like a teetotaler having a glass of champagne on New Year's Eve. It's merely irresponsibly amusing."

I scoffed and said, "Gotcha."

"So, in summary, Casey, as God, you have the power to do anything, but the wisdom, and ultimately the inclination, to do nothing."

"I see." I said, still with a hint of skepticism, drumming my fingers on the arm of my throne, thinking hard and Cerning the universe.

"What, Casey?"

"True or false – maybe I missed something – do all animals fight among themselves?"

"You know that's true. You didn't miss anything."

I continued to drum my fingers for a few seconds as I completed my computations. "While only about 0.3 percent of all mammals die in conflict with members of their own species, that rate is six fold higher, or about two percent, for primates. Even early humans, who were constantly at the brink of extinction had about a two percent chance of being murdered. That rate hasn't changed much to this day – on any world."

His face shrugged as he said "True. So what?"

"Well, I understand that murdering and being murdered is one of the most intense and gratifying Cerns, but if that activity were removed from the repertoire of activities, people would live longer and provide an even greater number of all other conflicts for us to enjoy. In fact, almost all religions seek to forbid their followers from killing. Why did I make animals so homicidal?"

He looked at me like a teacher who knows his student already knows the answer.

My face screwed up in confusion. I Cerned the universes once again to find the answer. I found that in every universe, in every conscious animal and conscience-bearing individual that had ever existed, homicide was an innate ability, if not unprovoked, certainly under adequate duress. But where did that inclination come from? Why would God include such barbarism in his creation? Certainly not solely for my own hedonistic pleasure! I was stumped. "Why is it there?" I pleaded.

He rolled his eyes with impatience, but remained silent and expectant.

"Ugh!" I massaged my head vigorously in frustration. There was no one else to Cern! Where was the answer? Then it hit me. There was one person I hadn't Cerned. Me, a.k.a. God. The answer must lie within! I dove deep into my eternal memory to that moment when I endowed the very first mortal beings with my own conscience. Some of them ended up murdering others! I was gob smacked! Completely flabbergasted! It had come from me! From God! I was the killer, the assassin, the butcher, the one who slaughtered trillions in millions of universes! I had bestowed upon every mortal being throughout eternity my own perfectly imperfect morality! I'd made everyone in my own image, not just visually, but morally as well!

The man was grinning with pride. His student had finally uncovered the secret of the universe. It was a powerful moment.

I was so excited! "I remember Bob saying 'little bits of God became everything'. All this time I've been thinking that it was only God matter that became people, and that's what was meant by 'I am God, and so are you.' But it's more than that! Everyone has God's morality, too!" I smacked my forehead in realization as I scanned liturgical writings across the universe. "Even in the Christian Bible, God is often depicted like a pre-pubescent psychopath with an ant farm! Flooding the whole world for Noah! Drowning all the Romans chasing Moses! Prodding to make people kill others because they were 'bad'! Ha! I was just egging them on for my own pleasure! Way too much prodding going on back then! It was like I had an amphetamine drip in my celestial arm!"

The man laughed out loud at that, but let me go on.

I became calmer as I completed my religious review. "But I'm also described as kinder, gentler God with a bellyful of butterflies who only wants humanity to surround him in one big group hug." I cocked my head in surprise and wonderment. "People are like that, too! Well! Paint me green and call me a cucumber!"

The head beamed with satisfaction, and with a conclusive nod said, "You passed. Enjoy your graduation tonight!"

With that, he vanished, leaving me floating there in my throne, saying to no one at all, "Thank you!" I looked around again, but everything appeared just as it did before my breakfast arrived. I want to talk to Jenna, I thought, but to my bewilderment, that didn't happen. Nothing happened. Was there something more to omnipotence? He said I'd passed the class. So, why did I not have the power to get out of this damned throne?

With the conclusion of that thought, fire erupted from every direction. Demons screamed past my throne chased by ghoulish, salivating, snarling hounds. I heard the wailing and anguished cries of millions. The acrid smell of sulphur filled my nostrils. My heart pounded with adrenalin and horror gripped me tightly! What in hell was happening? I saw Satan striding purposefully toward me out of the flames, walking on thin air. Horns, hooves, and a forked tail! What?! Suspicion replaced my terror. Lucifer approached menacingly, stopped about a foot from me, and said in a really evil voice "Welcome to 'Hell', Casey!"

The air quotes gave him away. "Bob?"

Instantly, the scene changed. Bob and I were standing on the front steps of the Omnipotence building. His costume was gone. "One of these days," he opined, "I'll really convince someone that they've gone to hell."

"Try being a little more original." I offered. We started walking toward the gate. "Besides," I added, "everyone who completes Omniscient school knows that God would never send anyone, much less himself, to such a place. No balance there. It would be as boring as heaven, if that existed."

"True that." agreed Bob. We passed through the gate and started up the path to the farmhouse. "Tell me," asked Bob, "what did you think of The OOO Academy?"

"Fast and furious! Immensely enjoyable! Wholly surprising! Fun and shocking! C'mon, Bob, do I have to recite every adjective in the dictionary?"

"I knew you'd like it!"

"You watch too much TV, Bob." He merely nodded. We walked in silence a while. After a morning of heavy-duty Cerning into multiple universes, it was relaxing and soothing to only Cern the immediate area.

The farmhouse was coming into view when Bob spoke again. "Do you have any last questions, Casey? Anything at all?"

I thought a moment. Bob knew I was omniscient, so why would I have questions? But, to my amazement, I found I did have one. "Who was the head?" I asked.

"Good job, Casey! That is the last question everyone asks. The answer eludes everyone. Don't beat yourself up over it."

"No, man, I won't. I'm just curious. Who was it?"

"You, of course."

"No, c'mon, Bob! Of course I'm everything including that head, and you and that llama over there, but whose head was that?"

"Beats me!" said Bob, "I've never seen him before. You conjured him up."

"I did?" I asked with incredulity. "I taught my own Omnipotence class?"

"Makes sense when you think about, Casey. Once you complete Omniscient school, you know everything, including how to teach Omnipotence."

I stopped walking and took his arm, turning him toward me, drilling his eyes with amazement. "But, but…how could I conjure without having the power to conjure yet?"

Bob shook his arm free and started walking again with a chuckle. I hurried to catch up as he explained, "Recall when you said 'Right now, I'm the maid.' there in the intake room where we first met and the mess disappeared? You've been omnipotent since the instant you arrived. You only needed to figure out how not to use it. Once you began Cerning history, you knew, it just took a while for you to put it all together. The instant you stepped out of that bedroom, you were the one making everything happen. Everyone does it a little different. I got to admit, I've never seen that combo before, though! A throne, a giant beach ball, and a head! That was really imaginative! But, yeah, the hell thing, that was me just playing with you."

I scoffed. "Yeah, you had me going there for a second or two…wait…one more question: why didn't I know it was you, you know, me being omnipotent and all?"

"Oh!" Bob looked at me in surprise. "Didn't Jenna tell you? Divine Beings cannot Cern into other Divine Beings. You can Cern a Divine Being's former mortal life, but once they get here, it's as impossible as it was to know another's mind while you were 'alive'." Silly air quotes.

I considered that for a moment as I noticed that an unfamiliar, saddled donkey was tethered to the hitching rail in front of the farmhouse. "So, there are two things God cannot do. Know the future, and Cern Divine Beings."

"Bingo!" said Bob cheerfully, then added, "It's a paradox – like being able to make a rock so big that you yourself can't lift it."

I looked at him quizzically.

"Just go with it. Hey! Looks like we have some company for the pre-grad barbecue! And if I recognize that donkey, you're going to love this one!"

Chapter 12: Picnic

Lively music was coming from the generous backyard of the farmhouse. Bob and I rounded the corner and were greeted by a festive crowd. A four piece acoustic band was playing an upbeat country tune, at least a dozen people were square dancing under a canvas pavilion, and many more were seated at several picnic tables, chatting and drinking from paper cups. A large pit fire was roasting a pig, slowly turning on a spit. Several folding tables were set with a large assortment of food. Several ten gallon urns labeled with their contents sat on a long table, and a large vat of steaming corn on the cob smelled enticing.

"Daddy!" squealed Abby, running toward me through the crowd. "Mom! Daddy's here! Everybody! Daddy and Bob are here!" She raced up to me and jumped up into my arms, nearly knocking me over. She hugged me hard and kissed my forehead as only Abby does, then jumped back down. "Jeezy weezy, Daddy, it's been almost a whole day since I saw you last! I thought you'd never get here! C'mon!" she tugged at my hand, "The hog's almost ready, and everybody wants to meet you!"

I laughed at her exuberance and infectious joy. "Ok! Ok, I'm here!"

Jenna came over from the corn vat, and we embraced comfortably, but briefly. "So," she asked, "can you do anything I can do?"

"Anything you can do, I can do better!" I sang in my best Ethel Merman impression, and we both laughed.

"We'll see about that one day soon! But right now, I need to fish those cobs out and soak 'em in some freshly churned salty butter! Abby, take your father around, and introduce him to our guests!" She planted a quick kiss on my cheek.

Abby rolled her eyes and said, "Jeez, Mom, if you guys are all done being mushy, that's what I was going to do!"

She led me around the yard introducing me as 'My Daddy' to the children and as 'My Daddy, Casey' to the adults. Someone gave me a cup of root beer on ice and a huge dill pickle. It was a bit strange, but I got the distinct impression that people were genuinely honored to meet me, like I was some dignitary or something, but I figured they were being hyperbolic to match Abby's enthusiasm. Everyone said they were looking forward to seeing me officially graduate at Crater Stadium later that evening.

At last, we came to a table where a man sat all alone. He wore a straw hat, bib overalls, and a closely cropped full beard. He reminded me of Amish men I'd Cerned. He was eating busily from a plate filled with potato salad, marshmallow and strawberry medley, marinated mushrooms, and fried chicken. He didn't notice Abby and I approaching until he threw back his head to take a long swallow of iced tea. When he noticed us, he coughed in surprise and a bit of tea spewed into his beard. He sat his cup down quickly, mopped his beard with a red and white checkered napkin, sprang to his feet, and exclaimed "Casey!" He was beaming with pleasure, and stuck out his hand for a shake.

I'd recognized all the other adults and most of the children from my historical Cerns, but not this man, yet he clearly seemed to know me. I took his hand in greeting and said, "I'm sorry, I don't recognize you."

"I'm Jesus," he said cheerfully, "Jesus of Nazareth! It is a pleasure to finally shake your hand!"

I recoiled in shock and yelped the interjection before I realized its veracity. "Jesus Christ!!"

"Yep," he confirmed, "The one and only!" He winked at Abby as he cackled at my response.

I was just standing there, eyes wide, mouth hanging open. Instinctively, I Melted back through history to the Middle East and found Joseph and Mary, the stable, and even the three wise men. I was able to Cern them all, but not the infant in the manger. I was flummoxed and pushed my omniscience for an answer. Just a half hour ago, Bob had said to me 'Divine Beings cannot Cern into other Divine Beings.' Understanding overtook my countenance, and I flopped onto the bench opposite Jesus. "Oh! Duh! Of course! You were never mortal!!"

"He's quick!" said Jesus to Abby. "I'm impressed!"

"You betcha!" beamed Abby, nodding, "Daddy's a top-notch student!!" Pride oozed from her.

"Indeed!" agreed Jesus. "Hey! It looks like they're carving up that hog now, Abby. Would you be kind enough to bring your Dad a plate of food while he and I have a little chat?"

"Sure thing!" Abby scampered off.

"I thought my donkey out front might have given me away." Jesus began.

"The donkey? It was curious," I admitted, "but it only makes sense in retrospect."

"I suppose so, but since everyone else popped in, you have to admit, it was suspicious."

I hadn't considered that there were no other means of conveyance about the grounds. No horses, buggies, bicycles, cars, trucks – not so much as a pogo stick. How did all these people get here? "No," I said, "what's suspicious is that there isn't a parking attendant out front, considering the crowd back here."

Jesus smiled and said, "Nah, Casey. Folks around here are lazy. They are more likely to pop than even walk to the refrigerator."

I shifted uncomfortably on my perch. I was omniscient, yet this man had just stumped me again. "Pop?" I asked, shaking my head in incomprehension.

"How do you think you got back to your bedroom last night? You popped."

I searched my memory. "Ohhh! You're right! And Bob! He does that stuff all the time! One minute he's there, then he just vanishes! Or vice versa." I added. "So, all these people really did just 'pop' in!" I chuckled with understanding. "But you rode your donkey here."

"Usually, I like to walk everywhere, but I stay quite a way from here." said Jesus matter-of-factly.

I nodded in response, not quite sure what to say next to perhaps the most revered person who ever lived. After a few more uncomfortable seconds of silence, I stammered with a laugh, "Look, uh, Jesus, I was never very religious, so I'm a little lost for words here. A biblical scholar would be far better company for you."

"Nonsense, Casey" he replied, "You're only beginning to realize everything you now know. You can recite the Bible word for word."

I Melted into the text for an instant and realized I could indeed. It raised a million questions I wanted to ask, but before I could settle on just one, Jesus began his message to me.

"It was a mistake, Casey, well, mostly anyway. I thought I could give the world hope, and I did – and still do – for a lot of people. It helps to maintain the delicate balance between good and evil, but as you've realized by now, I designed this universe so well, it didn't matter all that much. For every 'sinner' who changed their ways, I also influenced murderous, crusading armies that slaughtered millions, greedy religious charlatans who conned billions of dollars from sheepish parishioners, and way too many priestly pedophiles to name just a few of the colossally reprehensible consequences of my 'bright idea'!

"I was an imposter, Casey. A Divine Being, God Himself, who thought it would be sensational to appear to humanity as a mortal – walking on water, raising the dead, feeding crowds with a few fish and a couple loaves of bread, cheating death myself, and literally ascending to 'heaven'. Everyone was convinced that I was what I am, what we all are here. But it backfired, big time! Not only did my disciples and many others take liberal literary license in describing those events, but over the centuries, people argued over which of the largely fictitious accounts would be deemed as true. Just like you – and everyone else here – I am the Father, The Son, and The Holy Ghost – that Divine Spirit we impart to the newly conceived, and that which returns here after mortal death. We are that presence many people sense that is abiding and provides hope and moral guidance. But manifesting that spirit in a physical body and trying to explain to mere mortals was not worth it. I was about as useful as a fork in a sugar bowl! I caused as much grief as I did joy, and in the end, it simply didn't matter. As you've come to realize, there's nothing to be 'saved' from. People will act as they do, no matter what, in accordance with the free will that naturally provides us with all the enjoyment we'll ever require.

"The lesson I am here to teach you today is the last and most important Law of Omnipotence: Never, ever manifest yourself as a mortal. That's a can of worms that must never be opened again!"

His short lecture had been riveting, and considering the source, gospel – the absolute truth. As it had been while sitting on my own throne, I'd Cerned through history as he spoke and realized the full scope of hope and despair his presence on Earth had rendered. It had been an amazingly gratifying Cern, and I verified everything he said and much more. "I have a feeling you've delivered this lesson before – to more people than me. Do you meet everyone when they get here?" I asked.

He waved a hand. "Oh, no - only the very best and brightest. You're special, Casey - one of the best to arrive in a long, long time."

"I am?" I was incredulous.

He merely nodded and said, "You'll see. Oh, look! Here comes Abby with the food!"

Abby was approaching our picnic table gingerly, like a waitress: three plates balanced on her left arm, with two pitchers of root beer and ice in her right hand. "Phew!" she exclaimed, "I was so afraid I'd drop something!"

The plates were heaped with ham, pork barbecue, coleslaw, cobs of corn, glazed carrots, creamed peas, and collard greens. She sat with us, and we gorged to the brink of culinary coma. Abby chattered incessantly about three ducklings that had hatched that morning, a new quilt she'd been crocheting, and how Henry the rooster was terrorizing the hen house. Jesus and I let her ramble as we ate. Eventually, one of her friends came by and enticed her to join in a game of Duck, Duck, Goose that some of the older children were about to begin. She scurried off with him, and I rested my head in my hands, elbows on the table, and was content to watch the party.

The band played on, people danced merrily with practiced, yet carefree precision. The younger children played Hide & Seek among the crowd. There was face painting, balloon animals, cotton candy, and pony rides. Chickens, ducks, geese, cats, and dogs wandered the yard cleaning up fallen scraps of food. Laughter was abundant as were squeals of glee and joy. There was plenty of sunshine, no hint of rain. A warm breeze furled the tablecloths. It was the finest barbecue I'd ever imagined!

The shadows were growing long, and the crowd was thinning. People weren't saying goodbye, they were simply vanishing – popping away, as we say. Jesus excused himself and wandered back around the house. Jenna finally came over and plopped down next to me.

"Did you have a good time?" she asked.

"This afternoon was delightful. If I didn't know better, I could have believed it was the farm I grew up on. We had shindigs like this. I may never have to eat again, but, yeah, I really enjoyed watching everyone enjoy themselves!"

"You're such a wallflower, Casey!" she chided with mock rebuke.

"I know, right? I mean, I'm usually pretty gregarious, but I guess I just wanted to step back a little, given the last three days and all. It's a hell of thing to be murdered one day and God the next."

She smiled knowingly. "You'll get over it. Listen up, boyfriend; it's time to get ready for graduation. I took the liberty of laying out a nice set of clothes for you. Go grab a shower – you still smell a little like sulphur – get dressed, and we'll head on over for the ceremony."

Chapter 13: Graduation

When Jenna, Abby, and I walked out of the tunnel onto the field of Crater Stadium, I wasn't prepared for what my eyes beheld. To say it was gigantic would be an understatement. This place had to be what Jenna and I had been overlooking the previous evening. More than a million people were packed in carved out seats all around the spherical boundaries of the deep impression some ancient meteor had made in the landscape. From one rim to the opposite had to have been nearly a mile! The flat field at the bottom of the crater stretched the distance of ten football fields. The east side of the stadium was still bathed in bright sunshine while the west side was already in deep shadow. Several hundred folding chairs were set in a half moon configuration in front of a large stage in the center of the field, each of them holding a graduate of The OOO Academy.

The front of the stage was draped with a massive banner that read:

CONGRATS JANUARY 2020 GRADS!!

Behind the stage, an orchestra began a fanfare of celebratory music. A choir, dressed in lily white robes stood on risers behind the orchestra preparing for their cue. Large banks of lights facing the stage, and huge speakers and LED screens facing the crowd encircled the ceremonial center.

Jenna and Abby looked magnificent in flowing red matching gowns. I was dressed in a white tuxedo, gold bow tie, and shiny jet black shoes. The girls flanked me on either side; each had an arm linked with one of mine.

As we entered the field, the crowd erupted in deafening cheers, applause, and indistinct shouting. The screens showed the three of us walking along the gold carpeting that led to the center stage through the seated graduates. It seemed like we were the last ones to arrive, but were also who everyone had been waiting for. I was awe-struck and completely perplexed. I shouted at Jenna, "What the hell!??", but the crowd noise was so loud I couldn't even hear my own voice. It took nearly five minutes to walk the length of the runway. The orchestra played majestic parade music, amplified by the speakers. When the choir began to sing, the whole crowd joined in.

When God returns from his walk with matter, And rejoins Himself with us
He rejoins and we rejoice, With emotional Cerning lust!
Omnipresent omnipotence, Omniscient knowing all
We love ourself and all ourselves, no matter what may befall!
Take the oath! Eternity awaits!
Enjoy the show! That's all it takes!
From one came all and all are one!
Your life among mortals is done!

Jenna and Abby led me up the stairs to the stage. We stopped in front of three chairs setting to the left of an ornate dais and turned around to face the graduates just as the final flourish of fanfare ended. Everyone fell instantly silent. I shot Jenna a questioning glance. She nodded almost imperceptivity with a small quick smile and looked to the right of the lectern. Jesus was approaching it wearing a gold tuxedo, white bow tie, and shoes that matched my own. He stepped up to the microphone, raised both arms wide, threw his head back and proclaimed, "De Unum Multis!"

"De Unum Multis!" repeated the crowd with unworldly precision.

Jesus began his oratory. "I have gathered together here this afternoon to celebrate the completion of study pursuant to the curriculum of The OOO Academy of the eight hundred and seventy six souls who returned to ourself from Fulton County, Georgia during January in the two thousand and twentieth year of the Earth calendar. As you all know, this celebration, today's celebration is of special importance. We have among our graduates a milestone! Our number has grown steadily since we first breathed that tiny spark of our divinity into the first conscience-bearing being so long ago. Many of you remember the quadrillionth arrival just thirty seven years ago. Some of you recall the trillionth return nearly two centuries ago. Only a few hundred of you here today were present when we celebrated our billionth newbie, way back before I made my colossal mistake that we all nevertheless enjoyed so much." His voice trailed with chagrin.

Many of the crowd made short whooping sounds and several cat calls resounded throughout the stadium. Jesus grinned sheepishly, but motioned for the crowd to be still. "But today, our keynote speaker is our one quintillionth arrival! Most of you have probably focused a Cern on this man's mortal life by now, but if you haven't, I assure you, he's a class act, an excellent and quick study, and, in my opinion, the most imaginative and congenial Divine Being I've ever known! Ladies and gentlemen, I present to you Casey Dorchester Winsum of Atlanta, Georgia, planet Earth!!"

The crowd went wild with applause, whistles and cheers. The orchestra brass sounded a fanfare worthy of a king. The LED screens all showed a close-up of me!!! Five spotlight shadows rose and walked with me slowly toward the lectern. I was grinning like a fourth grade spelling-bee champ. I was astonished I could still be surprised.

"C'mon over here Casey!" shouted Jesus, beckoning to me.

The fanfare ended when I reached the lectern and seven canons reported from beyond the rim of the stadium in a perfectly-timed sixteenth-note septuplet. The crowd noise faded with the echoes of the explosive welcoming, and I found myself facing a silent, raptured audience.

"De unum multis." I said pleasantly.

The appropriate response from the crowd was distinct but little more than a murmur that dissolved into a void without the slightest cough. All eyes and ears were on me. The graduates fanned out before me. Most were adults, but at least two hundred were children. A quick Cern of their mortal lives revealed that most of them were, in fact, abortions. They were all from Fulton County, Georgia, as were the adults. They'd all died the same month I did: January, 2020, and had completed The COOO and OOO Academies within the past thirty days.

I addressed the graduates, "Some of us are brand new. I've only been here three days and two nights. A couple dozen of my fellow graduates are as new or nearly as new. Some of you have a few weeks under your belt."

I looked up at the crowd and turned in a slow circle as I spoke. "The rest of you here today have no doubt Cerned each of our formerly mortal lives and understand us better than our own Mothers. You have experienced our lives from conception to death. You've known our fears, our successes, our pain, our pleasure, and our quiet desperation. That desperation that resides in the pit of every mortal stomach is that rumbling in a mortal soul that constantly reminds one that one is, indeed mortal!

"You've Cerned each of our uniquely private searches for the meaning of life. You've noticed that this new batch of graduates is not unlike any other in that respect. While mortal, we vested our lives in a multitude of activities which we all assumed would improve our reputation, not just in the eyes of fellow mortals, but in the eyes of God Himself. In the course of that vestment, we provided all manner of enjoyment to our predecessors here. Little did we know what our purpose truly was!

"Mortals engage in every conceivable ideology, worship the strangest things, and perform acts that would make their concept of Satan blush. Mortals make decisions that cause great joy and happiness, but also horrible pain and mental illness. They celebrate. They suffer. They win. They lose. They help others. They hurt others. Every mortal is a turbulent ocean of delicious, satisfying, and immensely gratifying emotions.

"It is mortals who give God meaning. The meaning of mortal lives is to service God by simply living and making a thousand decisions every day that juices up their own emotion and the emotions of those with whom they interact. The simple act of going about one's day makes God happy. God is more than pleased to be every mortal. God is addicted to it. I am addicted to it. And so are you!

"But it's always worthwhile from time to time to remind ourselves of what it was like before there were mortal, intelligent, emotion-riddled beings. Think back, way back, before me, before you, before any of the universes to that time when I was alone. The sole Divine Being. Nothing else existed. Just me. There was nothing to Melt into, no one to Cern. I was alone, without purpose, and wondering what I was supposed to do about it. Think of the eons I spent in that vacuous dessert of existence.

"We must never allow that to happen again! We must do whatever we can to ensure that mortals always survive for it is their survival that gives us purpose and meaning! We are the ones who relish their misery, suffering, joy, love, and every little stupid decision they make! And it's so easy for us to do. To ensure the ongoing survival of mortals, the ongoing enjoyment by us of their lives, all we must do is nothing. I designed this universe perfectly. It's a self-maintaining and self-sustaining universe. It took many tries to get it right, but now it is, and all we have to do is not break it! Be modest in your prodding. Remain true to the oath to which most of you have already pledged allegiance and to what we graduates are about to swear. Just do that, and you will have eternity to revel in the lives of every mortal on every planet in every galaxy throughout the universe!

"In closing, there's one thing I want to share with you that was a surprise to me. Perhaps many of you, perhaps all of you will think it a parochial observation, but for me, I don't think there has been anything more surprising about being God than the degree to which the food around here is SO MUCH BETTER!!! Am I right?!!"

The crowd burst into approving applause with cheers and whistles aplenty. Jenna and Abby were on their feet clapping enthusiastically. "That's my Daddy!" yelled Abby.

Jesus was walking back up to the lectern, clapping and smiling. He wrapped an arm around me and delivered a quick hug. "Casey Winsum, ladies and gentlemen!" He took my hand and raised it high. "Our Quintillionth Divine Being!!"

The crowd rose to their feet and cheered even more loudly. The noise was deafening, but immensely satisfying. Dozens of banners unfurled throughout the crowd, all displaying:

1,000,000,000,000,000,000

I was being celebrated for something I had no control over. The standing ovation lasted many minutes. Jesus backed up a few steps to let me bask in my glory. All I could do was stand there, grin, wave back at the audience, and I must have said "Thank you!" a hundred times.

Eventually, Jesus returned to the lectern and motioned for the crowd to quiet down. They did so, almost immediately returning to the cough-less silence that had preceded my address. "Thank you, everyone," he said, "Now it is time for the reason we are all here. Administering the Supreme Oath tonight will be none other than the only other Divine Being that was never a mortal, the One who started it all, the mastermind behind the entire universe, the original and only God from whom all Divine Beings flow, the mind behind this perfect paradise, someone who greets everyone first, the Being I am so proud to call my Father, the Alpha and the Omega, Bob!!!"

The crowd exploded with wild cheering. Bob ambled across the stage and up to the podium. I took my seat between Jenna and Abby.

"Savory Cerning!" Bob roared at the crowd.

"Savory Cerning!" the crowd chanted back and then fell silent.

"All January 2020, former Fulton County mortals, please stand." commanded Bob.

All the graduates rose from their seat as did I.

"Raise both hands, and repeat after me: I do solemnly swear…" began Bob.

I and the graduates responded with precision after each clause.

"to abide by and cherish the Cannons of Divine Responsibility,…to refrain from utilizing my omnipotence to change the course of mortal intent,...to change the laws of physics,…to manifest myself as a mortal,..or to Cern another Divine Being….I take this obligation freely, without any mental reservation or purpose of evasion;… and I will well and faithfully abide with mortals from conception until death,… more often than not."

We responded with the last line with the same precision as always, but with a slight chuckle in our voices. Typical Bob. "Congratulations Graduates!" he roared again, "By the power vested in me by me, you are all Sanctified Divine Beings!!"

The stadium rocked with pandemonium. Cheering, whistling, shouts, and lots of jumping and waving came from every side of the crater. The orchestra launched into a strong, lively rendition of The Battle Hymn of the Republic, snares tapping, brass blaring, timpani pounding, choir singing:

My body lies a chillin in a dark cold morgue somewhere
It was posted and autopsied and was cut beyond repair
My organs were extracted only moments after I died
And now they're in formaldehyde!

Glory, Glory Hallelujah
I'll gladly Cern real fast into ya
You just live your life
While I witness all your strife
And we'll see you here one day!

Fireworks lit the sky, and the canons roared incessantly. Confetti rained down from nothing at all. The crowd poured onto the field to find their favorite graduate, or to simply dance and sing. It was a glorious celebration. The fireworks finale was as humongous as it was stunning. The sun had sat just as we'd taken our oath, and the night sky was a perfect backdrop for the display. Everybody turned colors as the various rockets burst in the air. Hundreds of people came up on stage to shake my hand and congratulate me on being the Quintillionth Divine Being.

Once the orchestra and choir finished their performance, and the last of the canon thunder faded away, people began popping away. Just a person here and there at first, but after thirty minutes, Crater Stadium was nearly empty. I shook the hand of the last admirer, turned to Jenna and said, "Man, oh, man! I think I'm getting callouses on my right hand. I shook so many!"

I noticed that Jenna, Abby, Jesus, Bob, and I were the only ones left on the stage. No one said anything, but Abby giggled. "Jeezy weezy, Daddy! Callouses make you more 'hand'-some." She used air quotes and batted her eyelashes impishly.

Everyone laughed at that. Bob seemed to have gotten a bigger kick out of it than the rest of us. He immediately began mocking the punchline, complete with signature air quotes, "'Hand'-some!" His laughter was unbridled, genuine, and loud. At first we laughed with him, but he carried on so long we began laughing at him, then finally, laughing at each other's laughter.

At last, we began to quiet down, and I collapsed onto my chair, breathless and a little weak. "So. That's it?" I asked no one in particular. Jesus and Bob glanced at each other as though they knew something I didn't. "What?" I pressed.

Jesus said "There is one more thing, but not tonight. It's been a long day, Casey. Dad says you've been to hell and back in the past twelve hours! You've got to be pretty exhausted and overwhelmed by now, so why don't we adjourn for tonight. Pop on home, grab something to eat, and get some rest."

I looked at Jenna. She smiled sweetly and nodded her consent. "Yeah," I said, stomach rumbling on cue, "that sounds like a really good idea. We'll see you tomorrow?"

"You bet!" said Bob.

I took Jenna's hand with my right and Abby's with my left. "Let's go home!" The next instant we were sitting around the kitchen table at the farmhouse.

The table was full of food and place settings. A large, steaming cheeseburger macaroni casserole was in the center of the table. On one side was a large bowl of tossed salad, and on the other, a sliced loaf of aromatic garlic bread. Large, frosted mugs of root beer sat in front of the plates.

One minute I had been saying goodbye to Bob and Jesus. An instant later, dinner was served. My eyebrows furrowed, and I cocked my head a bit looking askance at Jenna.

"I was too tired to cook. I just let it all – pop in." Jenna looked a bit embarrassed.

I scoffed and said, "What a marvelous skill! Works for me!" I chuckled at the convenience.

"Me too!" added Abby. "All that jumping and dancing has me just about salivating for sustenance!"

"That's quite a well-developed vocabulary you're employing!" I exclaimed, reaching for the salad.

Abby was scooping cheeseburger macaroni from the casserole dish. "I'm not a little girl any more, you know. Besides, I have over 40,000 dictionaries I've memorized so far."

"Well, then", said Jenna, passing around the garlic bread, "perhaps you know the meaning of pedantic. 'Salivating for sustenance' is too many words. I'm just 'starving'." She made a devilish face and reached for Abby's plate.

"Yikes!" squealed Abby. She covered her plate with her arms. "Stay away from my food!" She was serious.

Jenna and I shared a conspiratorial smile, but dropped the ruse; we were anxious to begin shoveling in some delicious food. As I ate, I reflected on the day's events.

"What do you think Jesus was talking about when he said there was one more thing?" I asked.

"Beats me." said Jenna through a mouthful of food. She chewed and swallowed, then added "After our graduations, that was it. We're all God now, so if there was anything else, you'd think we'd know it."

Abby piped up, "That's the one thing about this place that drives me crazy sometimes."

"What do you mean?" I asked.

"We can't Cern each other! How are we supposed know anything anymore?!" She actually seemed a little angry about it.

I paused the lift of a fork full of salad and said "But Abby, you and your Mom, and even Bob seemed to know what I was thinking many times during my lessons."

Jenna jumped in. "Not exactly, Casey. We had expectations based on experience. We've both schooled hundreds of newbies. You reacted fairly normally, and in many cases extraordinarily, but we were never certain of what you would do or think."

I thought on that a minute, then said "I think it's a good idea that we can't Cern each other. Besides, there doesn't seem to be much conflict or misery around here – in fact – everyone seems happier than a fat lap dog after dinner. Cerning Divine Beings would be boring, plus it would consume time better spent Cerning mortals."

Abby seemed surprised. "Dang, Daddy! You really are smarter than the average newbie!"

I smiled back at her and said, "Naw, sweetie, I just like surprises. That's all. Whatever the one more thing is, we know one thing for certain – it will be a surprise."

"Oh, my!" exclaimed Jenna. "Look at the time! It's nearly 11:00! I don't know about you guys, but I'm looking forward to my warm bed." She pushed back from the table and began clearing her dishes.

I glanced over at Abby. She was arching her eyebrows with an excited grin as though what her mother had just said was extremely good news for me. It took me a moment to put it together, and I felt a strange combination of emotions. There was no question that over the past three days, my love for Jenna had reignited. We had Cerned together our very own lives. That's a level of intimacy no mortal could ever come close to. Yet, just five nights ago, Alicia and I had made love, and even after nine years, it was as sincere as it had been on our wedding night. I hadn't had much time to think about her the past three days, but now, I missed her as well as Brenda. The prospect of sleeping with Jenna was a powerful attraction, but the guilt I'd feel might be something I would come to regret.

I finished off my frosted mug of root beer and belched loudly. Abby giggled. "Scuse me!" I blurted.

"Bring it up again, and we'll vote on it!" quipped Abby.

I rolled my eyes. "You need to come up with some new material, young lady. The first time I heard that, I fell off my dinosaur!"

"Sheesh! Look who's talking!" complained Abby.

"Hrmph!" I grumbled. "Well, I guess I'll pop back to my schoolhouse bedroom and get some shut eye."

"You can't." said Jenna. "Well, you can, but someone else is staying there tonight. Would you rather sleep with Alma Klozoff, or me?"

Wow, that was direct! My internal struggle must have been apparent on my face. My mouth worked around, but nothing came out. Abby giggled again. I shot her an annoyed glance.

"Trust me." said Jenna. Her smile was warm and inviting. "Go on! Go up and take a shower. Let me finish up down here, and I'll be right up!"

Chapter 14: On Beckon Mound

Jenna's bedroom was large. A four-post, queen-size bed, with a canopy, stood against one wall. It was made up with four pillows and what looked like an amazingly fluffy comforter. A long mahogany dresser seemed small against the opposite wall. A comfortable upholstered chair was in a corner with a goose-neck reading lamp behind it. There was ample free space in the room. The floor was covered with deeply piled, sky blue shag carpeting.

The shower felt great! It had a powerful massage setting that I let pound my shoulders and back for several long minutes. There was even a shaving kit in the shower along with a mirror. I took my time scraping off a three-day growth while the massage continued on my back. I shampooed my hair and used some marvelous almond scented body wash to cleanse my skin. For someone who wasn't at all sure about what he was going to do, I was sure acting like I knew exactly what I was going to do.

As I toweled off, I realized my body was in the mood to express itself, my mind, not so much. It was not in my nature to cheat. And it wasn't like Alicia would never know. Sooner or later, I'd have to face her. If the law of averages held true, it could be another fifty years before she got here. If I were to take up with Jenna, after fifty years, our relationship would be obvious to Alicia. And how would I explain Abby calling me "Daddy"? I stepped out of the bathroom, loins wrapped in a towel, into the bedroom. I was filled with indecision, uncertainty, a raging libido, and more than a small measure of guilt.

Jenna stood just inside the bedroom door, smiling warmly, dressed in nothing but a low cut teddy. This was not helping! We just stood there facing each other, about fifteen feet apart, nothing but shag rug between us. "You're going to love this!" Jenna said with muted excitement.

I stammered. "I don't know, Jenna. I'm not sure I want to do this. I mean, I love you as much – no – more than I've ever loved anyone, but I promised Alicia…" My voice trailed off.

Jenna was still smiling and nodding in understanding. "I know." she said softly. "But as a point of fact, you only promised her 'until death do us part', right?"

I chuckled nervously. "Yeah, but…"

"Relax, Casey. It is impossible for you to cheat on Alicia. Think about it."

I was baffled. What was she getting at? We were about to have physical sex! How is that impossible? My loins were urging me to get on with it! I shook my head and shrugged. "I don't get it!"

"Am I a physical being?" asked Jenna, her torso sitting on the floor and her legs standing beside it without a body.

"Holy shit!!" I exclaimed. "Jenna! Pull yourself together!"

She became whole again, and I understood. "We're spiritual beings! We can't have physical sex!"

She merely smiled.

"So, what are we doing here? Why have we gone through this pre-coital mating dance?" I was actually beginning to feel disappointed.

"Getting in the mood, silly!" She walked over to the bed and lay down on her back, her hands resting on her tummy. "Well, are you going to stand there all night? C'mon! Lie down!" I was as nervous as a long-tailed cat in room full of rocking chairs. I had no idea what was about to happen. My abiding reluctance coaxed one more "Trust me!" from Jenna.

I walked slowly to the bed, sat down gingerly and pulled my legs off the floor. I stretched out and lay my head back on the pillows, keeping about two feet between Jenna and I. "Now what?" I asked.

"We find two mortals about to have sex and Cern into them. I'll be the girl, you be the guy."

"At least that part makes sense." I chuckled.

Jenna closed her eyes and began her search. After a moment, she said with excitement. "Oh! I got 'em! I've been this guy before. He's a bit of a chauvinist, but you're going to love his mind. He's so poetic!!"

"Ok. Who is it? Who do I Cern?" I asked.

"Find 6528 Hollister Drive, Boise, Idaho. There's just the two of them there. Just jump right in to him, and I'll be her!"

* * *

There was silence, broken only by my own not quite steady breathing. Breaking my stance, gaze still lingering longingly upon her perfection, I eased back for a little larger point of view. There was no question, quite the quintessence of my own privately forged fantasy. My mind, mercifully, abolished time. I was free to study every centimeter of exquisite beauty my eyes now beheld. She will be held. My desire welled. Not brutally. Not indifferently, but differently. No comparison, just compulsion, compassion, compatible partners.

Her hair haloed her heavenly face; fine formed silhouette, not one out of place. It gently, yet jauntingly lay in layers; to her shoulders humble homage it paid. Her face quietly balanced, inviting, and serene. Contentedly, lovingly longing, silently singing a lean, a lonely melody,

Mellow and low; a basic belief held in her eyes that her heart may at last beat in peace. Her mouth mutely, perhaps mistakenly open. Words having been inadequate. Ample, full, yet inconspicuous lips silently beseeched my own to touch, not teasingly, pleasingly.

Her bare body blossomed below in a burst of celestial beauty. Breasts breaking the plunge of her neck, nestled nicely together, to gather them, gently, I must! Mermaid legs tapered to feet like fins, symmetrically placed. I braced myself. I must pace myself. I must face myself finally, fully, to measure my worthiness. Noticing fragrances fondling my nostrils, nestling resolve in my mind I found, fate will now place me on beckon mound.

Moving without motion we were nigh to each other, eyes fused, thighs mused, viable lovers were we. Only our lips moved, mutual motives, like magnets having no choice. Eyelids lowered, allowing our minds to meld, and at once all became moist. We met on a mysterious, yet comprehensive plateau. Our bodies would function in the art that we know. The answer now came, plain, not profane, sex had begun, but somehow not the same. We knew it was different, backwards at best. Bestiality abolished, laid finally to rest.

Our hearts in control, our bodies invoking our meld. Inviolate flesh, involuntary muscle's volition swelled till no muscle at all knew in what context it dwelled. Separate entities. Spirit and flesh and flashing sparks throughout the vicinity; we knew almost naturally we'd created a Trinity.

I watched and waited and wanted her now. Her skin was alive, undulating somehow. I saw my hand slowly, yet confidently rise, till my fingers brushed her nipple, as I looked into her eyes which rolled, relishing the sensation of inviolate domain at last destroyed; resistance fully waned. Her breast responded, resplendent with flush, burning and bristling, erect to my brush. Like a pulse of electricity, shocking and stark, we gave in to our bodies, closed eyelids left the room dark.

But tenderness tarries not for the meek, my hands slipped around her engulfing each cheek. Petrified as I was with a bulging erection, it slid deeply inward, no need for correction. Luxuriously lubricated, hot, taut, but not tight. Lightly I lowered her to the floor; she invitingly tugged at me wanting still more. Meeting each thrust with a push of her own, she caressed me and blessed me with each little moan. For her it was heaven, that space finally filled and I moved high upon her, and her clit was thrilled, not chilled, but sweating with heat, and she shuddered each time it and my dick would meet. Meaning and logic our loins blew asunder; each plunge to the depths rolled through our bodies like thunder. Under my body she rose each time, defying gravity my shaft she would climb. Faster and stronger my pulse did pound, cheering inside for at last I'd found, fate had just placed me on beckon mound!

Her heart beating wildly, blood in her ears was drumming. Excitement like this, and she still wasn't coming?! Her plateau had been reached yet somehow superseded, she wondered inside what the hell else she needed! Her cunt was afire and grew hotter still, she panted with pleasure, enjoying my skill. Jerking spasmodically she groaned for release; not wanting an ending, but yearning for peace. Rapid, rhythmic response from her hips was the rule, working in tandem with my hot, throbbing tool. Whimpering with pleasure, futilely hoping to relax, her orgasm was mounting and reaching its max! She fell silent, but tense as her nerves reached their peak, but they STAYED there straining, her cunt: wet and sleek! My prick like a piston continued to pump it. My dick wouldn't listen – it came , blaring - a trumpet!

The hot sauce shot to the ends of her soul, and finally she came from the depths of her hole. Convulsive twitching and sweating profusely, she brayed like an animal, somewhat Moosely! She couldn't believe the flood of release, but something was different - her excitement didn't decrease! My tongue in a flash was licking her clit, sucking that sausage and nibbling at it. A velvet warmth being all she could feel, she writhed there subdued like a beached electric eel. She was vaguely aware of this pioneer state in which she found herself at the brink of another orgasm, yet somehow sedate. Again and again she came with a moan, her body alive, her face simply shone.

My appetite finally satisfied with the meal, I began sucking her tits with a great deal of zeal. I fondled and flicked them and licked them with lust, those wonderful melons, that beautiful bust! She settled serenely at plateau once again, then asked me sweetly if I'd put it back in. So swollen it was I thought with alarm, if by putting it in I'd do her some harm. But leaping upon her much like a frog, that cavern easily swallowed my seven inch log. At once we both felt like heaven was here, we'd joined at the loins, Siamese Twins weren't as near. Together we moved in determined, steady motion, the lotion of love preventing friction. She playfully punned, "I sure like your dick-tion!" She giggled and quivered exciting herself much; the walls of her cunt - a vibrator to touch! The head of my penis swelled like a sponge, it felt like an onion each time that I'd lunge. This repetitive, expanding effect, this bulbous mass moving inside her caused her to gasp. Her nerves shot sky high, in a sweat she did break, her nipples stood up, her cunt began to bake! Her fever rose to an unprecedented height. She kissed me and scratched me and started to bite.

I doubled the speed of my hips. She lay back licking her lips. They were parched. Her back arched. The full length of my shaft now massaged her gloated clit. Clutching my hair, her breathing fell shallow. Marshmallow softness her cunt became. Gorged with excitement it puffed, swelling like a bullfrog's throat. Every vein, valley, and fissure of my fucking freight train frenetically found forbidden follicles of forsaken sensuality along the libatious lining of her labial lips. The corridor of her cunt was a sensitive as a tongue, and it unleashed a stampede of excitement that rushed to her brain like iron filings to an electromagnet. Her minds magnet automatically reversed polarity, and the tiny metal fragments shot to every micro millimeter of her body, warming it, comfortable, like a womb. She screamed, terrified that such ecstasy would surely send her straight to hell!

I exploded like an aneurysmal geyser. My steaming semen whitewashed the walls of her domain like a Spring flood gushing through runoff drains. Her vaginal valve opened completely, pleasurably, perspiration flushing my gushing gland with cool, refreshing wine. We floated to Earth as slow as a hot air balloon, drifting lazily down from ecstasy, to pleasure, to happy as hell.

Then slowly, ever so slowly, the rain diminished to a mist, then a fog, and finally I became aware of birds chirping and water running. Sunlight streamed through broken clouds, and the world was once again three dimensional. The buzz in my ears was gone, and my vision crystal clear. I felt I'd been born again. I lay on the floor savoring memory, listening to her humming a beautiful melody as she showers. The music, my heart it does fill. The singing, no longer longing, not low and mellow, but high and light. A bird happily, freely in flight. I think to myself after coming through this, that life is a pastime, but fucking is bliss. As I lay listening to this sweet serenading sound, I know in my soul that which is profound, there is no better place than On Beckon Mound!

* * *

The Cern dissolved. Jenna and I lay there on our own bed, beaming with satisfaction, merely holding hands. I breathed a long "Ooooooohhh! That was different! That was amazing! That was so unlike me, but oddly just what I needed!"

"I knew you'd like it! We call it Cerxing. You know – Cerning – Sex – Cerxing!!"

"Wow. I'd Cerned into people having sex yesterday, but with you in the other person, it was like I was both of them as well as each of us. Do you feel that way, too?

"Oh, yeah! Yes, I do!"

Chapter 15: One More Thing

Sunlight streaming through the bedroom window woke me the next morning. I could hear goats bleating in the distance and chickens clucking near the house. The aroma of sizzling bacon teased my nostrils. I realized that I felt fantastic. I couldn't remember when I'd slept so well. It was my first full day of being a full-pledged Divine Being. I was God, and I intended to carry out my duties faithfully. I looked forward to Melting, and Cerning, and Popping about. And, yes, maybe tonight Jenna and I could do some more Cerxing! I dressed quickly and nearly skipped down the stairs I was feeling so good!

Jenna, Abby, Bob, and Jesus were seated around the kitchen table. Platters of pancakes, waffles, hash browns, crispy bacon, biscuits, and sausage gravy filled the table. Abby was going around the table with a large pitcher of pulpy orange juice, filling everyone's glass. "Good morning, Daddy! You're just in time!"

"Morning everyone!" I said cheerfully. "Bob, Jesus, it's good to see you again!"

"Top of the day, Casey!" said Bob with a mouthful of waffle. He was working on his breakfast like a man with a plan.

"'Bout time you rolled out of bed, sleepy head!" chided Jenna, smiling intimately.

Jesus was guzzling his orange juice and was the last to greet me. "Verily, I say unto you today, thou shalt be with me in paradise." He cracked up at his own insincerity and spewed orange juice onto his bacon. He mopped his mouth with his shirt sleeve and belched.

Bob hung his head and shook it. "Jesus, Son! You always did have a keen grasp of the obvious! And mind your manners!"

Jesus looked dejected, then quickly smiled. "Sorry, everyone. Once you've been crucified, PTSD can cause some embarrassing behavior."

My appetite was ravenous, and I wasted no time filling my plate. I dug in and swore to myself that the food around here got better every day! Abby was chattering away about how she was going to make blueberry milkshakes with the goat milk she'd collected that morning.

I was using the last bit of a biscuit to soak up the last of the sausage gravy on my plate when Bob said, "I'm glad you're feeling good today, Casey. We have something we'd like to talk to you about."

I stuck the bite in my mouth, wiped with a napkin and said, "Sure, Bob. What's up?"

Bob snapped his fingers, and the table cleared instantly. The whole kitchen became spotless; as neat as one you'd find in a model home. "The nice part about messes is that they clean right up!"

"Good job, Bob!" said Jenna, "I hate doing dishes!"

"Anytime, Jenna. Anytime! You can do it too, you know."

"Sure – and I do – like last night's dinner, but I prefer old-school methods. I believe it helps to maintain my humanity." She nodded with affirmation.

"Whatever." said Bob with a hint of disapproval, but he turned his attention back to me. "Casey, when I realized that this universe was perfect – and that took several billion years until sentient beings developed – I began to play with an idea. We all get so much enjoyment from Cerning through the lives in this universe. I mean, just imagine it! One quintillion Divine Beings constantly abiding every mortal soul! It's a well-oiled machine! I always told myself that when we reached that number, I would know for sure, and I do."

I looked around the table. Jenna and Abby shrugged. Jesus looked like the cat that ate the canary. "What, Bob? What do you know?" I asked.

"I know we can duplicate it. Get twice as much bang for the buck! And I'm betting you just might be able to improve it." He leaned back with relief as though he'd just finished an overtime shift at a wildfire.

I wasn't sure I understood what exactly he was saying. "You want to make another universe?" I asked.

"No, Casey, I want you to make another universe."

I was shocked into silence. Abby exclaimed, "Do it, Daddy! Do it! We could have our very own universe!"

Jenna's face showed a bit of alarm. Jesus was giggling at our responses. I finally found my tongue and blurted out, "Me?!! You want ME to create a universe?"

"Yep. Number one quintillion – it's up to you! This is the 'one more thing'." He used his air quotes and smiled with satisfaction.

"But, but," I stammered, "I've only been here three days! What do I know about creating universes?"

"You saw them all Casey, while you were talking to yourself in that stupid beach ball. You saw every failure, and finally, the success. You know everything I know." he assured me, then continued, "Billions of years ago, I started the very first black hole. All this time it's been sucking in matter and compressing it into what is now ripe for another Big Bang. All it needs is your spiritual engineering."

"Spiritual engineering." I repeated.

"Sure. You get to tweak the blast to make it your own. I know you'll take care to not break your oath, but I think you will create something fresh and even more gratifying than this universe."

I puffed my cheeks and let out the air slowly as I raked one hand through my hair. Just a week ago, I was racking my brain preparing my closing argument for Jake Ramos, and now I'd been tasked with the creation of a universe! I considered that when God asks you to do something, one should probably do it.

"What if I blow it?" I asked tentatively.

Bob waved a dismissive hand. "I doubt you will, but even if you did, there are thousands of ripening black holes out there. We'll catch another one soon. You can try again."

Jenna slowly raised her hand like a student in a class. "What, Jenna?" I asked.

"Does this mean you have to go away, like, forever? A whole universe to take care of – that's got to be a 24/7/365 job!"

I didn't know. There was no precedent in history for this. I turned to Bob with the question on my face.

"It will take about a week to set it off, but once in motion, it will self-sustain, just like this one. It will exist as a parallel universe, and Divine Beings here will be able to Melt and Cern into it and vice versa – once intelligent life develops - but that will be billions of years from now. Perfection takes time. Imagine it, though! Twice as many mortals! Surprisingly fresh Cerning! It'll be a blast!! All Divine Beings will be able to move freely between both universes. You all could have homes in both universes if you like."

Well, that didn't sound so bad. Already, I was beginning to get some ideas about what I might do with my own universe. "What do you think, Jenna? Can you do without me for a week?"

Jenna sighed. "I waited over eleven years for you to get here. I suppose another week won't hurt, much. But really, I think it's a wonderful idea! Such an honor, Casey! You'll be the first former mortal to create a universe and the first Divine Being to ever create a parallel universe! That's a two-for if I ever heard one!"

"Then it's settled?" asked Bob, "You'll do it?"

"Do it, Daddy!" urged Abby, "Can you make me some sharligators?"

"What's a sharligator?" asked all four adults simultaneously.

"You know," explained Abby, "A cross between a shark and an alligator! Grrrr!!" She made a ferocious face and started thrashing about in her chair in an utterly comedic fashion.

Leave it to Abby to lighten the mood. We all laughed, and I said to her "I'll see what I can come up with, Abby." I winked at her, and she beamed with appreciation. "When do I start?" I asked Bob.

"No time like the present. Just a few instructions though. Be sure to Melt back through the five most recent Big Bangs paying particular attention to the blast dynamics, the alignment of elements, and the trajectory of the blast wave. In the last Big Bang, take particular note of how carbon is used to initiate life. It is within that engineering where you will make your changes to give us something familiar, yet deliciously fresh."

"That's it? That's all the instructions?" I was surprised.

"That's it! See you in a week!" He and Jesus vanished.

"I know just the place for you to do your work, Casey." said Jenna, "The sun porch at the back of the house is away from the animals. You can settle in there. Abby and I will bring your meals, but will otherwise leave you to work."

"Sounds good!", I said. "Something tells me I won't be getting much sleep for the next week, so I don't think I'll need a bed."

"Follow me!" said Abby. She led me through the house to the sunporch. It was a generous area, enclosed by screens. It faced south so it got sun nearly all day long. There were three padded wicker chairs and a long low table. The floor was covered with thin outdoor carpeting. A collection of long-handled farm tools hung on the wall of the house. A spring-loaded screen door let out into the backyard.

"This will be just fine, Abby! My attention will be elsewhere, so comfort is not a priority."

"Make a really good universe, Daddy! Don't forget the sharligators!" Abby skipped away into the house.

Chapter 16: Forging

Other than spending the nights at the schoolhouse, and that time in the beach ball, this was the first time I'd been alone since I'd left the intake room. So much had happened in just four days. It was right about this time of the morning that my head had been blown off. Had it really only been eighty four hours ago? Life as I knew it had changed so much. I was God. I had seen, Melted into, and Cerned everything in this universe. I had gained intimate familiarity with billions of mortals, the entire body of mortal knowledge, a clear and honest view of history, including thousands of universes that preceded the present, and I'd gained a daughter and Divine Lover. I'd been celebrated as the one quintillionth Divine Being, and now, God Himself had chosen me to do something no one had ever done before: create a parallel universe.

I relied on my firm belief in my own omnipotence to guide me through the task. I paced the sunroom as I created a mental to-do list for myself. When I was satisfied it was complete, I sat down in one of the chairs, leaned back, closed my eyes, and cast a Melt all the way back to the fourth to last Big Bang.

I found the mass of matter, just moments before it exploded. It took several minutes to Melt entirely into it, despite my skill. It wasn't big at all, perhaps the size of a basketball. But it was so dense! The space between protons, neutrons, and electrons was all but nonexistent. There were as many elemental particles in this mass as there were in the entire current universe – all packed in a small rock! This is going to take a while, I thought.

With the speed of God, I began to analyze the mass. I determined percentages of all the elements, noting how they were separated or congregated throughout the mass. At last, I'd mapped the entire blob and not a second too soon. It was already trembling and emitting more heat than ten super novae. I felt Bob's presence manipulating the process, but there was no communication. I was mesmerized as I watched the matter begin to transform, elements and compounds were shifting within the mass. The trembling turned violent, and then there was a massive explosion that flung particles millions of light years in less than a millisecond!

Whoa! Let me go back and slow that down! That explosion was way too fast to tabulate all the data I needed. I Melted back one minute and slowed time to a snail's pace. Each nanosecond of the explosion now took a million times longer – an entire centisecond. Yes! This was much better! It was like looking at ultra-high speed video, one frame at a time, one hundred frames per second.

At this much slower speed I could easily track each and every particle as they were flung into space. It was at that speed that I got my first glimpse of something I hadn't noticed in previous Melts. At this stage of universal birth, there was instilled in every last particle, a Divine intent. It was fascinating to watch inanimate matter behave in accordance with a mission. Elemental particles instantly were attracted to both like and unlike particles. Countless masses of varied composition formed and separated themselves from other masses. Most of them were merely gaseous, but many began to form solid molecules and compounds. Huge deposits of hydrogen began to fuse into helium, and stars were born. I focused on the solid masses that took up orbit around the stars and found several that held all the elements required for life to evolve. I wanted to see, with absolute clarity, the precision of allocation of elements that would ensure the result of reproduction.

My omniscience was growing by leaps and bounds. I considered that just because you know everything doesn't mean you can't learn anything new. Every centisecond I was presented with a tsunami of data that had previously been unavailable to me!

The Melt of that fourth to last Big Bang took me several hours to complete, but by the time I dropped out of it, I was confident that I understood the fundamental process by which a universe could be created that would produce and sustain intelligent life.

When I opened my eyes, the sun was well on its way to setting. Two sandwiches, a pile of potato chips, and a large mug of root beer sat on the table before me. Naturally, there was also a plate of Pop Tarts and a note from Abby:

Hi Daddy!
Here's some food for you. I know you are working hard and making a really fun universe!
Don't forget to eat!! Love you LOTS!!!
Abby XOXOXO
P.S. Don't forget the sharligators!

I loved this child so much! I was indeed famished. Being God must require a lot of calories! It seemed that eating was one of the things Divine Beings loved to do, even though it was entirely unnecessary. It wasn't like we could starve to death. Perhaps it was like Jenna preferring to cook instead of just popping out a dinner. It helps to preserve our sense of humanity – a sense of normality.

I woofed down the sandwiches and snacks. I was anxious to get back to my project. I wanted to Melt through the entire history of that fourth to last universe to see exactly how life began and where it went wrong. With the last Pop Tart in my hand, I settled back in my chair munching the pastry as I Melted back into the ancient universe. First, I fast-forwarded several billion years until the first intelligent life evolved, then I back tracked through the evolutionary path to the point of the very first living cell. I dove deep into that cell, analyzing every particle, and became an expert on RNA and DNA construction. I moved forward in time and watched that first cell evolve into more complex organisms. I watched with amazement as the RNA mutated every so often to produce something brand new. Eventually, life evolved into plants, then animals, and finally intelligent beings. But those people were more violent than not, and they struggled to maintain their own numbers. Ultimately, they destroyed one another, and that universe was consumed by yet another gigantic black hole.

I dropped out of that Melt after much less time than the first. My skills were improving! But the Melt had raised more questions for me. What caused the RNA to mutate? How did Bob control that? How did the RNA manage to affect the entire countenance of intelligent life? I needed to see the next three universes to gather data to compare. Hopefully, that comparison would yield the answers I needed.

The next three Melts went much more quickly than the first; I knew what I was looking for! The RNA was the key to everything, and I had to discover the means by which I could manipulate it. I isolated all four instances of the first living cell and compared them. They were identical. They all started with the exact same coding. I moved forward to the first mutation of each. In each of them, different chromosomes changed! So, how did that happen? I focused on just one chromosome and ran the change over and over looking for that instant, that event that initiated the change. I had to keep slowing it down as it appeared to change without cause. It happened so fast!

Finally, I slowed it enough to see what was happening. Just before the code changed, the chromosome pulsed with energy, and I could feel the will of God making it happen. In two instances, he turned off a gene, and in the other two, he turned one on that had been dormant. At the same time, he'd installed what I can only describe as a program within the RNA that would ensure the proper sequence of mutations and the proper times to complete the evolution to intelligence.

Huh! So, I really only needed to do two things. Create a proper explosion, then wait for life to evolve and implant the evolutionary instructions! The laws of physics maintained everything else.

In the three universes preceding the present, the intelligent beings were also flawed. In one, they seemed to find reproduction disgusting, and although they mandated it, people still failed to perform. Eventually, they died off. In the second to last universe, people turned out to only live about 25 years, their telomeres were way too short! Unable to sustain population growth, they soon died out as well.

In the universe before the present one, people were shy, reticent, and uninspired - a total snooze-fest for a Divine Being seeking emotional highs.

The evolutionary instructions Bob had implanted in each universe were very much alike, but I could see which chromosomes he was trying to get right. When I finally Melted into the first living cell in the current universe, I saw the perfection that he'd finally worked in. People lived as long as three generations or more and were balanced in their violence and compassion as well as their complacency and ambition. I figured it out! I could duplicate what Bob had done! But could I improve on it?

When I stopped Melting, the porch was dark. The moon was full and bright. The dishes from Abby had been cleared and replaced with a plate of meat loaf, mashed potatoes, and green beans. Fresh root beer and Pop Tarts were also there for my pleasure. I was hungry, but also in full manic project mode. I wasn't tired at all! I wanted to get back to my task immediately and nearly decided to forego the food, but Abby's note still lay there – reminding me to eat. The meat loaf was delicious! It never ceased to amaze me how good the food was around here!

Next on my to-do list was to find and analyze that small dense mass that would become my universe. I thought this part would be relatively easy, but it proved more frustrating. It wasn't difficult finding black holes; they're hard to miss! The problem was there were so many of them! The vast majority of them were small and just beginning to accumulate matter. But there were at least three dozen that at first glance could have been the one I was looking for. I ended up having to Melt deep inside each to measure their density and weight. I was looking for the heaviest and the densest of all. My patience was wearing thin, but I was determined, and at last, I found it sucking in matter near one of the oldest and far flung reaches of space. It proved to be slightly larger and denser than the mass that had produced the current universe. Finally! I drew back a little to look at my little universe egg. I felt like a mother hen!

From this one little ball of everything, I was going to create an entire universe! It was beyond ripe and beginning to quiver, so I'd have to work fast! First, I had to do a deep analysis of the mass. I found that its composition was not unlike all the previous ones, but the percentages of elements were different. It contained a little more hydrogen, a little less oxygen, and considerably more carbon than the others. But like the others, the heavier the element, the scarcer it was. Relatively speaking, any element with more than sixty protons could only be found in traces. And they were horribly mixed up!

With a single mighty act of will, I corrected the alignment of the mass to produce the proper blast. Once aligned, the quiver became a tremble, and the heat rose astronomically. It was going to blow any second! I double-checked the alignment quickly to ensure it was correct. I was concerned about the different percentages of elements, but my guess was that they would produce sensationally new and different objects that would knock the socks off of everyone.

I released my Melt from the mass, and it exploded in a cataclysmic blast that flung matter into a new universe.

Instantly, there were more new places to Melt into than there had been just a second ago. I was absolutely ecstatic! I was mesmerized as I watched my handiwork begin to form into stars, planets, solar systems, asteroids, meteors, comets, and more than a few sights no one had ever seen before. To my delight, space was no longer pitch black, it had a bit of a purple hue to it that reminded me of eggplant. In the wide expanses between the developing galaxies spewed massive colorful fountains of multi-colored gases. Unable to tear myself away, I watched the formation of my universe hour after hour. Everywhere I looked was something surprising, beautiful and magnificent. Galaxies were forming, but they were smaller and more numerous than those in Bob's universe.

To someone who'd never seen a Big Bang before, it would have seemed like frenetic chaos, but my universe was compiling exactly as I'd planned, and much the same as its precursors. I'd done it! I'd created a universe! I was God!!!

"Casey?" Jenna was shaking my shoulder gently trying to bring me out of my Melt. "Casey!" She shook me harder. I didn't want it to end. "Casey!!!" she shouted.

Reluctantly, I fluttered my eyes open and released the entire Melt.

"There you are!" said Jenna. "We were beginning to think you'd never come back!"

I looked about at the boring screen porch and the yard beyond. The grass needed mowing, but other than that, it was the same, serene and familiar scene it had been when I started. I began to speak, but realized my throat was as dry as a dessert. I pushed forward in the chair, poured a mug of root beer, and chugged it down. At last, I could speak. "How long?" I asked.

"Nine days! After six, we started getting worried. But you were sitting there smiling and occasionally groaning with pleasure, so we let you go. But by this morning, everyone was Melting into your new universe! We knew you were done, so I figured it would be OK to pull you out."

I blinked several times. "You've seen it?" I asked incredulously.

Jenna's face lit up like a Christmas tree. "Yes!!!" she squealed. "It's incredible! Consummately stunning! I only spent a few minutes there myself, but I can't wait to explore it in great detail! Bob has already put a governor on Melting into your universe. Absolutely everyone is transfixed by it, and he was afraid no one would be left to maintain abiding Cerns in his universe, so everyone is limited to one hour a day to Melt into yours."

I laughed happily. "That's pretty cool! Everyone's seen it, huh? And they really like it?"

Jenna mocked denial, "No Casey, they LOVE it!!! You did a magnificent job, boyfriend!"

"Well, it's a start," I agreed, "but the real test will be if I can create intelligent mortals that will exceed the pleasure we derive from those we have now. But that's like, several billion years from now."

Jenna snorted dismissively, "Ha! What's a few billion years compared to eternity? It'll be here before you know it. Besides, at just an hour a day, it will take everyone that long to Melt into all of it."

"Yeah," I agreed, "it's a lot bigger than this one, and the chemistry is a little different. There's plenty to learn just by Melting and Cerning the inanimate."

Just then, Abby came running out of the house into the sunroom. "Daddy!! Daddy!!" she ran up to me and launched herself into my lap, flung her arms around my neck, and hugged so hard I nearly choked. "You did it Daddy! I knew you could!! I just spent five minutes there, and it is absolutely wonderful!!"

"Well, thank you, Abby! I'm glad you're pleased with my work!"

She released her death grip, pushed back from me a little, and leveled a stern stare at me. "You didn't forget about my sharligators, did you?"

"Um, no, Abby, I didn't forget, but that's going to take a little more time. We have to let the new universe cool, condense, and begin to cook." Her little face fell with disappointment. Her lower lip began to quiver a bit. "Oh, Abby, don't be sad! You'll get your sharligators. I promise!"

"When?" Her brow was still furrowed with displeasure.

"Not long. Maybe three or four billion years." I tried not to emphasize 'billion'.

"Four BILLION years??!! I'm only eleven! That's forever!" She pouted.

Jenna stepped in. "No, sweetheart. YOU are forever. A billion years will go by just like that!" She snapped her fingers.

I was all the talk for several months after that. People kept coming by the farm, bringing all sorts of gifts and food dishes, to congratulate me and gush about how good a time they were having in the Casiverse. That's what they started to call it. There was now a Casiverse and a Bobiverse. They'd Melt one and Cern the other. They all said in so many words that the Casiverse was the greatest thing ever.

Many visitors made suggestions about what kind of life and what kind of intelligent beings there should be. One guy wanted rhinoceroses striped like zebras. Another wanted flying monkeys like in The Wizard of Oz. A sweet older woman, who'd been a neighbor of Noah, wanted the people to have gills. Several younger women suggested I have people lay eggs instead of giving birth. Liberace stopped by one day and tried for a half hour to convince me to put seven fingers on each hand. Bob Ross wanted pink trees. Kobe Bryant stooped in the door one Sunday morning with an autographed basketball for me, and suggested that I consider making hamstrings twice as powerful. There were more sinister suggestions as well. Cyclops, six legs, an instinctual craving for cocaine, forked tongues, huge ears, and eagle eyesight for precision shooting to name just a few.

Abby maintained her lobby for the sharligators and came up with a few new ones: a turducken, a docat, and a bunnygoat. I assured her, and everyone else, that I would give their suggestions serious consideration. But I was in no hurry. I had billions of years to craft my lives, and I was determined to make them spectacularly pleasurable to Cern.

Chapter 17: 3,428,112,952 Years Later

The Bobiverse was really getting boring. More and more Divine Beings mentioned the monotony of Cerning what had by now become the nearly predictable lives of all too familiar mortals. With the popularity of the brand new Casiverse, it was still a challenge to keep Divine Beings focused on the Bobiverse. While the population of the Bobiverse had tripled over time, our Divine population had multiplied by a factor of over ten thousand. Many of the oldest solar systems in the Bobiverse were being consumed by their cooling and expanding stars which provided spectacular mass casualties that were still satisfying enough to Cern, but all that delicious gloom, despair, misery, depression, agony, and death was nevertheless becoming unsurprising and banal. Cerning was getting stale and crowded! It was not uncommon to have a quadrillion people Cerning the same mortals at any given time, and Divine Beings were clamoring for fresh emotional highs.

With Divine Spirits low and some even languishing for lack of Cerning surprises, everyone was tasked to be on the lookout for the perfect combination of elements and environments that will provide the seed into which I would breathe life. Everyone felt the urgency to develop a new crop of remarkably extraordinary mortals; my Casiverse was the only hope. I was their only hope. If I got it right, we'd have the first newbies in another two billion years or so.

Alicia and Brenda were here, of course. Alicia showed up fifty three years after I did, Brenda 27 years later. It seemed like they'd been here with me forever. Brenda had had seven children who had been just as prolific. I had more descendants than would fit in Crater Stadium. It had been a little tense at first, between Jenna and Alicia but it didn't take long for them to become fast friends.

Surprisingly, Cerxing with other men became Brenda's favorite pastime. Here, everyone loved everyone.

We all still lived on the farm. It had been remodeled countless times and was more than adequate for Alicia, Brenda, Jenna, and I. When she became a young adult, Abby had moved a short distance away. That's when she decided to stop aging and become a zookeeper. She kept a bungalow on the grounds, but often came over for dinner. She was still sweet and childlike. All the abortions stayed that way. Their exuberance for being was unflappable.

I'd long ago settled on the genetic tweaks I wanted to install when the time was ripe in the Casiverse. I kept it a secret, though, in case my calculations were incorrect. As long as it turned out at least as good as the Bobiverse, I could always say, "Yep! That's just the way I planned it." But I was hoping for much more. I wanted to bedazzle everyone!

One of the rooms I'd added to the farmhouse was what I referred to as my laboratory, but it was really just a place where I could work undisturbed. I fashioned it much like the throne in the beach ball, except the boundaries were transparent. People would often stop along the road to observe me floating on my throne, deeply emerged in a Casiverse Melt. If they were lucky, they would happen by on one of the occasions when I'd conjure up an alter ego and argue with it.

About one hundred and fifty years after I created the Casiverse, a really sharp VR newbie dude by the name of Chip Skalor showed up and offered to build a virtual reality addition to my laboratory. It took nearly a thousand years to perfect, but in the end, I was able to run simulations of various genetic modifications to see what they might lead to. Over two million years, I tried more combinations than a Lockmaster factory until I was as certain as possible that what I had settled on was the genetic code that would seed my Casiverse. Nevertheless, without knowing the future, it was impossible to be absolutely confident. So, for the last three billion plus years, I'd been sitting on the code waiting for the primordial soup to come to a boil.

Today could be the day. Reports of prime conditions had been pouring in over the last three months. Hundreds of planets were ripe for life. I'd calculated that I needed, to be on the safe side, at least a thousand planetary incubators. I'd spent the past ninety days verifying the reports, while still looking for new ones myself. Yesterday, the count had been 992. Most of the planets fit for life had been found at the furthest reaches of the Casiverse. They'd cooled and formed first. I'd started there and worked my way back, finding fewer and fewer the newer the planets were. But today I had a hunch. There was a small, relatively young galaxy that was filled with smaller than normal stars. Perhaps their planets had cooled faster without the heat of the supergiants that populated so much of the Casiverse.

I Melted into the galaxy and began methodically searching the billions of stars, looking for those with planets in the Goldilocks zone – not too close, not too far from the star. For the first twenty minutes, all I found were balls of lava and liquid gases. Then, BINGO! I found one! And then another in the same solar system! 994! I'd never found two so quickly before and never in the same solar system! Was this a fluke of my universe or had I just hit the motherlode?

I popped off my throne into the barn where Jenna was forking hay into the horse troughs. "Jenna!!" I shouted. Jenna jumped so violently she dropped the pitch fork. I'd completely ambushed her with my presence.

"What??!!" she shouted back, clearly annoyed, shaking herself like a dog to rid the terror I'd just delivered.

"You gotta help me! I think I just found the motherlode of suitable planets!! I already found two in just twenty minutes, and we only need six more! The two of us can knock that out maybe by lunch time!! It's just one galaxy!!"

"Really?!" Jenna was smiling. She knew me well enough to know I was not one to cry wolf. She was as anxious as anyone about finally having fresh and exciting new Cerns to enjoy.

"Yes!! Yes!! This could do it! Will you Melt with me? Right now?"

"You bet I will! I was almost finished here anyway. Let's do it!" Her excitement was as keen as mine.

"Follow my Melt!" I urged.

Jenna followed me to the galaxy I'd found. "This is it." I said. "See that little yellow star and the third and fourth planets?"

"Oh!! Yes!! I see them!" She Melted deeper. "The soup and environments are well within parameters!" she exclaimed.

"Yes!! Now, you go toward the far rim of the galaxy, and I'll work my way into the center. Let's see if we can find more."

We fell silent as we Melted throughout the little galaxy. For several minutes, we found nothing.

"Got one!!" Jenna nearly leaped off the floor. It was the first one she had ever discovered.

"995! Just five more! Keep looking!" I coached. Before I finished speaking though, I'd found another myself. "Whoa Buddy! I got another one! 996!!"

"Here's another one!" shouted Jenna. "And another!! I can't believe it!! I just found three planets for you!!"

"Oh, Jenna! You're not going to believe this!! Jump to my location!"

"Ohhhh!!!" cried Jenna, "Look at THAT!!"

"Yes! Oh Yes! FOUR planets in the same orbit around one star, all prime for life!! That makes 1,002!!! We did it!!" I took Jenna's hands and danced a little jig with her, both of us laughing like we'd just gotten a pardon from the governor ten minutes before execution. Indeed, if my code worked, our Cerning enjoyment could become something no one, not even God Himself, had ever imagined.

"I bet there are more in this galaxy!" I said with excitement. "Let's get everyone we can find to do a thorough search of this galaxy and see how many more we can come up with!"

We both popped out of the barn to gather more help. Thirty minutes later, Bob, Jesus, Brenda, Alicia, and Chip had all joined us in the barn. "With seven of us, this shouldn't take long at all!" I addressed the group. "Follow Jenna and I into our Melt. We'll show you what we've found, and then we'll fan out and complete the galactic survey."

Two hours later we'd found sixty two more prime candidates for a total of 1,064. We were all as excited as school children on the last day before Summer vacation.

"Alrighty, God Almighty!!" exclaimed Bob. "The day has finally arrived! I know you're ready, Casey. We'd sure like to watch it happen. Do you mind?"

"Not at all! In fact, I would be honored to have my dearest friends witness the birth of life in the Casiverse."

"Wait!! Wait for me!!" Abby came running into the barn. "Sorry I couldn't be here sooner, Dad, but Mr. Holcomb brought in his pregnant sow who had a breach going on. What did I miss?"

"Not much" I feigned nonchalance. Then my face lit up. "Just the discovery of seventy two new prime-for-life planets!!!"

Abby squealed and pumped a fist to the sky. "Yes!!!" She knew what it meant.

"I'm ready to implant the code and everybody here is going to watch. You in?" I asked.

"I wouldn't miss it for a whole plateful of Pop Tarts!!" shouted Abby. "Do it, Daddy! Do it!!!"

"Ok! I'm going to talk you all through it. Join my Melt. First, I locate each of the 1,064 planets and maintain a simultaneous Melt. The next step is to find the very best location that contains all the elements we need to construct the genome. We zoom in to the molecular level. See all those genetic molecules floating around aimlessly? I'm going to put them together like a jigsaw puzzle, making two identical strings. This will take a while. There are over 17,000 pairs to mate. The first 2,000 or so are those that will eventually turn into flora, the second 2,000 will become fauna. Most of the remaining genes contain switches and instructions that tweak size, shape, color, internal biology, external limbs, and intelligence, as well as the timing for all the necessary changes and mutations that will result in a huge variety of living things as evolution occurs."

The group watched, mesmerized by my skill. After all, I'd done this a million times on the VR. But this one was for all the marbles. After a few minutes I'd arranged all the pairs. There was just one thing left to do: turn it on.

"Ok. The 1,064 pairs are finished. I'm zipping and twisting them…and now…I AM GOD! IT IS MY WILL THAT YOU SHALL LIVE!"

The group gasped as each one of the chromosomes pulsed with the spark of life. It took less than three seconds for them to divide and reproduce themselves.

"It's working Daddy!!" whispered Abby.

"Look at them grow!" exclaimed Jenna, "They've already divided 16 times!!"

I was feeling utterly magnanimous. I had created life. I had become God!

"Well done, Casey!!" Bob slapped me on the back. No higher praise was possible than that from God #1.

I was beaming like a spotlight!

"What now, Dad?" asked Abby. "When do I get see my sharligators?"

"Well, Abby, if my calculations are correct, you should be able to dissect one in about two billion years. Intelligent primates will take another billion, give or take." The group looked at me like I had just given them a free lunch but charged for the plate. "What? C'mon guys, you all know that evolution takes a long time. I'm a God, not a magician!"

Jesus giggled.

Chapter 18: 2,459,348,112 Years Later

The Sun had swollen as it squeezed the last of the hydrogen from its core. It had swallowed Mercury and Venus over the past 200 million years and was nearing Earth. Life on Earth was extinct; burned to ashes long ago. The once lush and beautiful globe now was little more than rock and dust where it wasn't covered with lava flowing from massive cracks in the Earth's crust. While the population of the Bobiverse had continued to expand, our number of Divine Beings were so many it was usual to find hundreds of trillions of Divine Beings in any given mortal at any given time. The last time I'd asked Bob how many Divine Beings there were, it took him a full 30 seconds to recite the number. I never asked him again. Whatever the number, there was growing angst among them. With so relatively few mortals to Cern, everyone was limited to just two hours per day. One thing we'd learned over the eons was that having too many Divine Beings Cerning the same mortal at the same time was a bad idea. It made them lethargic, indecisive, and apathetic, which rendered Cerning dull, boring, and unfulfilling. Our dissatisfaction with the now overwhelming monotony of familiar Cerning became even more pronounced and desperate. Still, it was all we had, and everyone was jonesing for much more.

On the bright side, the Casiverse had flourished. After the initial seeding, we found more and more compatible planets as the years passed, and now, more planets had life in the Casiverse than had ever had life in the Bobiverse. We could still Cern history as much as we liked, but it was like watching a favorite movie for the millionth time – enjoyable, but you already knew how it was going to turn out. It just wasn't the same as live Cerning where everything was a surprise.

Everyone spent the bulk of their leisure time Melting my creation. It was fresh, new, and subtly, but brilliantly different. They marveled at my genetic engineering that had produced quietly fluorescent royal blue grass whose tips evaporated at exactly two inches releasing a marvelous scent that bathed the landscape. The loved the vines that grew into complex, canopied mazes all by themselves. Giant weeping willows with cascading layers of multicolored fronds stood like umbrellas over wide meadows full of magenta daffodils with blooms that opened or closed every ten minutes creating an undulating wave effect that was hypnotizing.

There were billions of species of insects, fish, reptiles, and birds – all sporting bright colors from every coordinate on the light spectrum. Many of them were chameleon-like and could blend in flawlessly with nearly any background. Abby was in animal heaven! Her zoo was a hundred times larger and held magnificent specimens from all the new worlds, including her long-wished-for sharligator. Rainbow colored quadrupedal mammals, ranging from tiny to monstrous roamed, preyed, and groomed the vast land masses on each planet. Fresh water shot from continual geysers everywhere creating shallow, but expansive pools below them that were chock full of skittle-colored fish.

I remembered thinking that watching a pot of water come to boil seemed to take forever but waiting for primates to develop large enough brains had been excruciatingly slow and laborious. They'd first appeared over 500,000 years ago, and finally, they had reached the point where it might be possible to implant their souls. I was pestered all the time by Divine Beings begging me to pull the trigger, but I was determined to wait until at least seven planets had a population of at least 100,000. The primates had figured out that living in caves was better than trees, but fire and the wheel still eluded them. They were primarily herbivores, but would eat fresh, raw meat when the opportunity arose. Their language was still largely gestures and a variety of grunts. They'd developed small communities, never larger than thirty members, but would not hesitate to injure or even kill one another over territory, food or a mate. They had consciousness, but they had no conscience.

But what my people did have was the topic of every conversation! My coding endowed them with phenomenal telescopic eyesight that could perceive wavelengths well below and above the normal 280nm to 780nm range that people in the Bobiverse were limited to. They could see everything from ultraviolet to infrared and were able to look a mosquito in the eye at 1,000 yards, and count the eggs laid by an African driver ant from three feet away. Their sense of smell was as keen as a dog's, and they could hear a spider spinning a web. They never got sick either, unless they ate something poisonous. I'd boosted their immune systems to fend off any virus, bacteria or microbe that invaded. The cancer genes had been completely eliminated. There was one more big surprise that I held in reserve and would only become apparent after many years of Cerning.

When the Casiverse had developed its lush flora, both Brenda and Jenna had gotten in the habit of joining me in my laboratory each day. They each chose their own version of my throne. Brenda floated on a beach lounge while Jenna conjured up something that resembled a large high-backed motorcycle seat. She said it reminded her of riding a horse.

We'd started today by Cerning into the population of San Francisco on April 18, 1906, starting a few minutes before the big quake struck. To re-experience all the terror, pain, suffering, heroism, compassion, and love that filled that day so strongly was satisfying, but, alas, a rerun. Still, it was enough to keep us going. After stopping for a quick lunch, we settled in for our daily Melt into the Casiverse.

I melted into Prime 3 and did the count. "I've got 23 more! Primate population is now 136,417. Brenda, how's Prime 2 today?"

"Hold on a minute…one of the tribes pulled up stakes last night. Oh! There they are. Ok, let's see…it's flat." she said dejectedly. "Still holding at 139,333."

Jenna chimed in, "Prime 1 picked up 44! We have 167,518!"

"Great!" I said, "Let's move on to 4, 5 and 6."

After a minute or two, Jenna exclaimed "Wow! Prime 4 had 37 new births in the last 24 hours and no deaths! It's at 106,418 now!"

Brenda chimed in next. "Prime 5 only picked up 6, so that makes 101,017. Still above the threshold!"

"That's good news. We don't need another tsunami knocking them back under like it did last year." I said as I finished my count on Prime 6. "I've got 100,791 on Prime 6 today. Alright then. You know the drill – all of us count Prime 7 to be sure we don't miss anyone."

"I'm going straight to the cliff dwellers on Horseshoe Bay! Most of those pregnant women were in labor yesterday! That hurricane last winter resulted in a lot of hanky panky!" said Brenda.

"Yeah", said Jenna, "they could have delivered enough, but those idiots on the peninsula were still fighting and killing each other over that hippabeast carcass!"

"Let's just get in there and count. No point in speculating." I said. "Let's do it."

All three of us bore down on Prime 7 scouring the planet for primates, counting as we went through every valley, plain, mountain, jungle, beach, and cave.

"I got 100,014!!" shouted Brenda.

"Me too!" Jenna said with excitement. "Casey??"

A slow smile overtook my face as I confirmed their count. "Yes. It's 100,014!"

Then all three of us shouted in unison "We have seven planets!!"

My Casiverse had been cooking for 5,887,461,064 years, and it was finally ready for my Divine Soul! Only the three of us knew the threshold I'd set. And I was the only one who knew what else was about to change. This was going to be a surprise to over a googol Divine Beings, many of who would be engaged in a Melt when I installed conscience in these primates. They'd feel it instantaneously, and these creatures would be inundated with Cerns immediately. I was about to fulfil the long-held hope of every Divine Being.

"Well?" asked Jenna, "What are you waiting for?"

"Just savoring the moment, Jenna. This will be the most spectacular day I've ever had. An accomplishment like this is something I've looked forward to for so long, I'm not sure I want it to be over with. Once I do this, my work will be done. What will I do with myself for the rest of eternity?"

My two dear women looked at me like my head was on backwards and shouted a chorus at me. "You enjoy it, silly!"

"Jeezy weezy!!" added Jenna, looking away with annoyance.

"Ok! Ok!" I laughed. "Of course I'll do it!"

Brenda and Jenna floated their chairs over to mine and faced me, each of them taking one of my hands. I looked at both of my loves and thought there was nothing I'd ever experienced that matched the confidence these two had in me, and the love that flowed from them. It gave me strength and determination to do what only Bob had done before.

I closed my eyes and said "Hang on tight, follow me in, and prepare yourself to witness something no formerly mortal being has ever witnessed before!"

I established the Melt slowly (for a God) and deliberately. I took up firm residence in all 851,508 of the primates on all seven Prime planets.

"FROM GOD'S SOUL YOU RECEIVE YOUR SOUL AND YOUR PURPOSE. I GIVE YOU CONSCIENCE WITH FREE WILL!"

The three of us watched with amazement as a subtle change rippled through the countenance of every primate. They paused whatever they were doing, looked frightened for an instant, and then shuddered. They all looked around frantically as though seeking the source of some disturbance. Finding nothing, they slowly returned to whatever they had been doing.

Jenna and Brenda couldn't help themselves. They Cerned into several primates immediately. I remained in the Melt and dove into each of their genetic codes to see if the last secret gene had turned on as I had programmed it to do when at last a soul was installed. Yes! It had worked!! It would take several generations before the mutation would be apparent. I wondered who would be the first to realize what I'd done.

Jenna and Brenda had slumped back into their chairs, eyes focused a billion miles away, enraptured. Soft moans of pleasure, surprise, and delight would escape them every few seconds. I resisted the powerful urge to join them. There would be a hundred trillion years or more to enjoy the Casiverse, I'd have ample time. Instead, I popped out of the laboratory and into Bob's house. He and Jesus were in the same state that Jenna and Brenda were in. I popped over to Abby's bungalow, and she was spread eagle on her bed, eyes shining, wholly emerged in novel Cerning. I checked everyone within 25 miles of the farm. Every last one of them was deeply emerged, suckling the fresh milk of brand-new emotion.

It had taken about twenty minutes to survey the immediate locality, and by the time I popped back into the farmhouse kitchen, Bob was sitting at the table chewing a mouthful of T-Bone steak while busily sawing off another bite. He glanced up at me and nodded at the plate he'd prepared for me. "Dig in!" he said and went back to sawing.

I scoffed with a crooked smile. Two Gods pop into a kitchen and eat T-Bone steaks. Had to be a joke in there somewhere, but a punchline didn't occur to me. I sat and began to eat, suddenly realizing I had a ravenous appetite. Nothing new about that.

Bob studied his food until it was gone and then took a long swallow of iced tea from a huge goblet. I'd remained silent and patient while I ate. Bob mopped his mouth with a napkin and leaned back in his chair, finally leveling his gaze at my own. "I saw what you did, Casey." His expression was placid, neither angry nor pleased.

I paused an instant, then placed the last bite of steak in my mouth. I wasn't sure about which part of what I did he was referring to, but I had a feeling he saw the genetic change. I stretched my lips into a hopeful smile as I chewed, but my eyes remained apprehensive.

"While everyone else was jumping into Cerns, I stayed in your Melt." he said evenly. I opened my mouth to speak but he raised a hand to stop me. "Don't worry, I won't let the cat out of the bag. I won't even tell Jesus."

I searched his face for some sign of evaluation. He sighed, glanced away then back at me with a beaming smile. "That was brilliant!!! Not only have you reinvigorated the entire community of Divine Beings for the foreseeable future, but you've probably amped up our pleasure by tenfold or more! I couldn't have done it better myself! You are every bit a God as I am! It is an honor to call you my equal. You are no longer becoming God. You have become God. You ARE God!!"

Tears of happy pride streamed down my face. God Almighty Himself called me His equal!

Chapter 19: One Last Surprise

140 Years Later

The Casiverse was thriving. Over 2,000 planets now were inhabited by conscience-bearing beings whose number exceeded 100 million. Before that first day was over, Bob had amended the Divine Oath from limiting everyone to two hours Cerning the Bobiverse to a requirement of at least four hours. The Casiverse was so attractive, almost no one preferred the Bobiverse. That was unacceptable. No mortal may go a nanosecond without at least one Divine Being Cerning them. God must always be with mortals, lest the soul be lost. Bob had never lost a soul, and he wasn't going to allow the new car in the garage to gobble up all the gas. The Bobiverse contained over 100 trillion mortals, and they deserved our attention as much as those in the Casiverse.

Divine Beings had been so Cern-starved, they'd barely left the developing primates except to eat and sleep. One of the enhancements I'd programmed into the Casiverse was to fix the log jam in mortals that occurred in the Bobiverse when too many Divine Beings were Cerning a mortal. The lethargy it produced in the Bobiverse wasn't occurring in the Casiverse!

Interaction in the community fell off sharply. Everywhere you looked people were comfortably lounging as they Cerned the new worlds. I'd spent thousands of days Cerning the magnificent people I'd created. They were bright, fast learners, and passionate in their pursuits. Their conflicts were brutal, but their will to survive was immense. They fiercely defended their families and community, but were expeditious in eliminating transgressors. The emotions were much more intense than any I'd felt in the Bobiverse. Each Cern was like riding an uncontrolled bottle rocket. They were thrilling, always surprising and utterly addicting. Abby got to the point where she had to set an alarm clock to pull her out of her Cerning each afternoon, so she would not neglect her animals. Every day she'd bring back the blueprint for a dozen new species she found, so she could conjure them into her zoo.

Jenna and I were having a late dinner of pot roast with potatoes and carrots, macaroni salad, and green fried tomatoes after a long day of Cerning.

"I was Cerning people on Prime 1 today." she said.

"Mmhm" I muttered through a mouthful of food.

"I noticed something a couple years ago, and today I just had to look."

She knew! She'd discovered the secret Bob and I had kept all these years. But I played it cool with mock nonchalance. "What did you have to look at, Jenna?" I asked a little too evenly, after swallowing.

"There are people there now who are 50, even 60 years old."

"So?" I asked.

"No one down there looks a day over 35."

"Really?" I feigned disbelief.

She looked at me like a mother who knew her child was covering up. "Don't be coy with me Casey," she warned, "I Melted into their genome today, and I saw what you did!" Her tone had change completely. She was excited!

I couldn't help but smile, but maintained my ruse for one more time. "What did you see Jenna?"

"These people are going to live 300 years or more, if they don't get themselves killed! Now, all by itself, that wouldn't change things all that much, but with their super-senses and quick intelligence, I can't wait to see what kinds of things they discover and invent by the time they die! What if Mozart had lived to be 300 years old? We'd have ten times as much of his music to listen to! What if Einstein had lived another 200 years? He might have been able to prove his Theory of Relativity! But these people – they WILL live another 200 years. Think of all the extra, and more mature, and therefor NEW emotions we will experience! It's just going to get better and better and better!!! No one will ever want to stop Cerning the Casiverse!"

I took a long draw of root beer, mopped my mouth with my sleeve, smiled at Jenna with all the love I had, and simply said, "Imagine that!"

#

Thank you for reading my book. If you enjoyed it, won't you please take a moment to leave me a review at your favorite retailer?

Thanks!

Amanda B. Reckonwithe

What's Next

Being drafted now is the sequel to "Casey - The OOO Academy" in which the entire realm of Divine Beings is threatened with extinction, in spite of their Godly abilities. While the premier novel is relatively benign, the second installment will explore the darker side of the inhabitants of the Divine Community. It will shatter the age-old beliefs of God Himself.

About Amanda B. Reckonwithe

Amanda B. Reckonwithe was born into a poor, but hard-working neighborhood on the outskirts of Wheeling, West Virginia in 1978. She grew up exploring belief systems on five different continents while writing poetry, fiction and fantasies about life, death, religion, black holes and cosmic coincidences. She died briefly in 2017, when she gained insight into the afterlife that became the basis of her first novel, "Casey - The OOO Academy". Amanda now lives on a sprawling, wooded and secluded Montana mountain with five cats, a cockatoo named Phydeaux, and the only sharligator in captivity that she calls "Death". When not writing novels, Amanda likes to hike trails or speed race through the forest on her Mongoose Excursion mountain bike.

Contact Amanda B. Reckonwithe

amandabreconwithe@gmail.com

www.ingramcontent.com/pod-product-compliance
Lightning Source LLC
Chambersburg PA
CBHW051952220626
47052CB00004B/915